A
Tropical
Depression

A
Tropical
Depression

Richard E. Wentz

iUniverse, Inc.
New York   Bloomington

Author Photograph by Bernard Levy @ bernard-levy.com

iUniverse books may be ordered through booksellers or by contacting:

iUniverse
1663 Liberty Drive
Bloomington, IN 47403
www.iuniverse.com
1-800-Authors (1-800-288-4677)

ISBN: 978-1-4401-7545-9 (sc)
ISBN: 978-1-4401-7544-2 (ebbok)

Printed in the United States of America

iUniverse rev. date: 02/03/2010

Forward

————◆•••◆————

I STARTED WRITING this story before Katrina hit and finished it the Christmas after. In the intervening time, virtually every place I knew growing up in New Orleans; every school, every playground, every house of my friends, every restaurant and "po' boy" place, every bar, every landmark of youth, adolescence and adulthood that I made sure to see whenever I returned (almost every year after moving away in 1990), was taken by the water. For certain, some areas survived, downtown and French Quarter the most prominent of those. But as a true local, I rarely visited those areas when I lived there and only stopped by for either beignets and coffee at Café du Monde or breakfast at Mother's on Poydras Street on my return visits.

It is for certain that some facsimile of New Orleans is emerging from the destruction caused, not just by the storm, but also by the years of negligence from scores of politicians; local, state and federal. New Orleans has been flooded more than once in it's history, and like before, it will re-build, but it will not be the New Orleans I knew for more than forty years. More than likely it will be a somewhat violent Disney cartoon version. The vision of people who don't know the city, but somehow think they know it.

Don't get me wrong, prior to Katrina; New Orleans was by no means some form of the Emerald City. Its politics were as corrupt (or probably worse) as now, its streets dangerous, its public schools a disgrace, and the rest of its city services horribly underfunded. The only thing the city had going for it were its people. Who when needed, banded together, put up their own money

1

and started charities and non-profit organizations for almost every facet of city life. From education to cleaning the parks to keeping the performing arts alive in a city that has had according to its own tourism website"live entertainment for over 250 years". It has been the people who have made a difference. Which is, I suppose as it should be, because it was always the people that made New Orleans what it was in the first place.

There are references to places; bars and restaurants in my story and they are all based on places that my family frequented. One in particular, the Po' Boy Bakery, owned by Gary "Koz" Gruenig has relocated to Harahan, Louisiana (6215 Wilson St., Harahan, 737-3933; www.kozcooks.com) and is now called "Koz's".

Find it, say hello for me, eat a roast beef "dressed", drink a cold Barq's and enjoy a small sliver of a civilization lost to a great deluge much in the same way as ancient Atlantis.

REW/ New York City, January 21, 2009

For my sister Peggy Matson.

Without her encouragement, timely financial help and most importantly her love and advice this story and so much else of my life would not be possible.

One

---·•·◦·•·---

I AM AWAKE. That much is certain.

I know I am awake because my head hurts like a son of a bitch, and my head never hurts when I am passed out.

I know I am awake because the pain in my head makes the tin roof sound like the mad hammering of a thousand wooden mallets wielded by a thousand demented Gepettos. And I never hear the rain when I am passed out.

I know I am awake because above the hammering rain, I hear my Times-Picayune newspaper hitting the screen door with a tremendous "whump", before it bounces once off of the sagging wooden porch and into the struggling azalea bushes, where it lands with a slosh. Against my better judgment, but in dire need of a cigarette, I attempt movement. This is done by reaching my right hand slowly over the top of the empty Borden Milk crate that serves as my nightstand in a touchy feely search for my cigarettes and lighter, and in the process, sending a plastic "go-cup" half filled with watered down gin and tonic spilling onto my clothes, which lie in a heap next to the bed. I force my eyes to open, manage only slits, and wait anxiously for the expected and deserved shoots of pain to explode in my forehead. Ahh, there they are.

As I lay in bed listening to the rain soaking the paper and echoing throughout my rented narrow shotgun house that I continue to use to get away from everybody who happens to know me, I consider carefully the dread that has on most of the days since childhood, blanketed the purgatory of my mind. That grey area I tend to retreat to between what is conscious and what is un-conscious, its great weight forcing a constant frown on my face. This dread has slowly spread over the last thirty years to create a sort of mental ground cover that hides most of, but not all of the weeds of self-loathing that sprout within me on a daily basis. Self-loathing that has become increasingly easier for me as I have gotten older, stemming from the nasty combination of a thousand or so years of a repressed Protestant bloodline - well-practiced in the art of martyrdom - and the fact that I have begun to decay. Becoming a paunchy, quickly graying broadleaf miserable-for-the-most-part, forty-year-old man who has spent the lion's share of those forty years, except for one brief, ill considered marriage, alone.

The mere fact that for the past few months the events of my life have been such that until very recently I was able to wake up in the morning, throw the covers off, look down at myself and not see complete wretchedness was an achievement unto itself. But now, while lying sprawled on dirty sheets that loosely cover a paper thin and coffee stained Salvation Army mattress, in the bedroom of what began just two months ago as a "pied e terre" rented to make things more convenient for myself and my then girlfriend, I begin to realize that my small hideout has now become a dank hole to crawl into now that life has become more than a little dicey; thrown me a curveball, if you like baseball references. This place allows me to hide away from the dust-covered relics of a life I still exist in, but no longer live .

Taking a drag from the cigarette and tapping the ashes onto my pile of clothes I think about how this particular fist-fight with myself was set in motion yesterday afternoon at my office. I had just finished a meeting with Sylvia Griffin from the New York office, no "looker" by any stretch, but what the hell. I was looking for a grudge fuck and she was looking for…god knows, but nothing ever materialized because I heard the news that I knew I would hear eventually and the day got away from me. I tore my emotional stitches open with a long night of gin, tonic and the blues provided by Walter "Wolfman" Washington… the self same dread that I speak of this morning… that I had managed to hack and beat into submission for a short while, had crept back into the forefront of my every thought, and every second of my waking hours like the Kudzu vines that blanket and choke the oaks, the cypress and the telephone poles that line the highways outside of the city.

I am at my rental house on this rainy morning to escape; naturally, since it is what I do best. I am a classic avoider. When things are normal, a state of being I am having a hard time recognizing lately, I stay at my three story 1920's bungalow I purchased in the Uptown section of the city; near Tulane University on Jefferson Avenue, a couple of blocks towards Claiborne Avenue and just North of Freret Street. Bought with the blood money gained with the bonus I got for taking one of my minor advertising clients national. Cue

Announcer: "A necessary household defense system for these dark days of the War on Terror "that not only cleans but kills germs, even Anthrax". My "real" house is the very house I shared with my wife every single day for 3 years and 352 days, until the day she decided she didn't want to share it any more and instead opted for greener pastures in the manner of a grotesque four thousand square foot prefab bit of an eyesore in Metairie. Which just happened to include our former couple's therapist, her new boyfriend, therein. I personally don't go to Metairie. I didn't as a kid, except for a couple of times to party in "Fat City" when I was in high school, and not as an adult. Metairie is the suburbs, the home to the thousands of white flight families of the 1970's and 80's who thought that the final destruction of New Orleans was foretold by the election of increasingly blacker administrations. But what those people, and the others like them (namely my parents) who fled for similar bastions of white security North of Lake Ponchartrain failed to remember or realize is that race has always held a backseat to money in this city, and that the black administrations, learning from the white, continue to cater to the wealthy while pissing all over the poor, black and white alike.

I digress. I have that tendency.

Anyway it was after that meeting with Sylvia, while I was blissfully chain smoking cigarettes (that as I lay here smoking, promise to myself to give up yet again) and standing on the expansive veranda of the large oak shaded Garden District home that some idiot converted years ago first as a hotel then as a suite of offices, that I learned from one of the secretaries, Bernadette Champion, of the final and complete return of my former lover and current co-worker Jessica Maris to her former and apparently now current husband Stephen. Who happens to be a nice fellow if you try not to consider that he is from all accounts, (as I have heard, but in truth never actually met the man), the very definition of an asshole. And if it may please the jury, may I present that he is the same guy and same marriage Jessica left over a year ago after he disclosed his undying devotion to her. Well, not actually to her, his undying devotion was to another woman.

"Jess…" Bernadette drawled between drags on her American Spirit, "… was on the fence about re-marrying him but gave in after he bugged her constantly and finally agreed to seek anger management counseling."

'How magnanimous of him', I wanted to snarl, but Bernadette, a stickler for details, and a true gossip aficionado, went on.

"Evidently, Jess paid for both of them to fly out to Vegas over the weekend, where they re-married in one of the quickie chapels, not the Elvis Chapel, but one of the others. Then they spent the night gaming, drinking and watching shitty porn in room 7512 of the Aladdin. Though Vegas does have that new porn that lets you pause and fast forward and stuff, so maybe it wasn't that shitty"

I was…I don't know what I was, or what I still am as a result of hearing that dandy bit of information, about Jess, not the porn. I remember losing my breath and that Bernadette and everything around her seemed to fade out of focus. In what must have been my first out of body experience I found myself easing backwards to the railing of the porch, looking to it for the support that I knew my legs were not going to give me any more. I gripped the railing like a madman, but, and here's the Protestant for you, I managed to endure the rest of the time outside on the porch without Bernadette seeing my anxiety, which rose in me like a river of bile-filled lava, cresting at the sealed summit of the volcano, and like Mount St. Helens, searching for the thinnest layer of crust to burst through. Afterwards, once back in the safety of my office, the other twenty or so employees of J. Thomas Hunt Advertising didn't seem to notice the change in my tone the rest of the day. Or that I diverted my eyes whenever Jess walked into a room that I was in, or that I crept out of the office at four forty-five instead of my usual six o'clock so that I could avoid seeing or talking to her. In fact, after having spent the afternoon building a fine wall of hate and self-loathing, I could've cared less if I talked to her ever again, a tough but not impossible task even though we both work in the same department at a small agency. I left through the back door of the office, preferring to climb over piles of garbage in the alley than running into anyone who may in the course of a one or two word conversation hear in my voice the fear accumulating inside of me. It was a short drive down St. Charles to Napoleon Avenue where I turned left towards the river and Miss Kate's, my comfort and salvation. A venerable New Orleans institution that is no more than a hole in the wall that has had the good fortune to play host to my drunken tirades so often that they have become as much a part of the place as the 25 cent claw machine.

My first memories of drinking as a kid of sixteen are of Miss Kate's, not the big place she is in now (her needing to move as a result of a fire started when an old drunk fell asleep on the floor next to a six foot stack of yellowed Times-Picayunes). But of the original, no bigger than a walk-in closet, and made more crowded by the improbable pool table greased and jammed into the back half of the bar. The front door of the old place had a one foot square, two-way mirror cut into the top of the door at eye level that allowed the bouncer or Miss Kate to turn away anyone that wasn't to their liking, usually local blacks or Tulane rugby players. Drinks in the old place were served in seven ounce plastic cups, consisted of mostly alcohol, regardless of the mixer and cost only seventy-five cents. On Wednesday's, believe it or not they were two for one. As a kid I could go in with ten dollars and count on throwing up in the backseat of Mitch Brook's '68 GTO. The drink priced "jumped" to a buck and a quarter to help Miss Kate cover the cost of the move. The regulars complained at first, but they, me included, still show up. My main reason for loving the place though is the amazing juke box. A Pleistocene holdover from the days of 45's that spews the great history of New Orleans music from Louis Armstrong to Fats Domino to Allan Toussaint to The Neville Brothers. And then there's Miss Kate herself, a Crescent City icon with her ever-present Pall Mall cigarettes, suspicious cat's eye glasses and mountainous blonde beehive hair-do that commands the type of respect only found in southern beauty and funeral parlors. She speaks in the true New Orleans accent that reminds people more of Coney Island than Canal Street, calling oysters "ersters" and lengthening single syllable words almost beyond recognition, as in "Ya want anutha bee-yah honey?" Her age is a mystery, and to ask, the highest insult. To those that know her, she has a permanence that matches the river itself. To me, she has been here since the city was founded and she will last until it washes away in that as yet great un-named storm.

As I slammed my 5th or 6th Boodles and tonic down my tightening throat, I casually announced (louder than I thought I was) that this was indeed going to be the official beginning of the end of me. I decreed that the night had been conceived in and designed while driving there, around drinking. But not simply drinking socially, quaint, tidy with pinky finger pointed to the ceiling. Last night was dedicated to the art of drinking with anger and with the sole purpose to get drunk. Not exactly the quest for the grail but having been born and raised in the one city in the world where drinking alcohol is considered as natural as breathing, where in fact if a person is known not to drink they are as often mistrusted as a Massachusetts Democrat, it is as noble a quest as any attempted by knight, Templar or not.

Not one of the ten or so patrons of the fine establishment moved.

They didn't care, largely because they were probably there for the same purpose, but with their own reasons. New Orleans embraces the drunk, the good drunk that is, the happy Otis from Mayberry drunk. So much so that if, inconceivably, a person has decided after years of drinking to actually stop entirely and become "sober" as they say; and after they have stopped drinking that same person falls under the impression that he or she will be lauded, and thereby reveals their new sobriety to others, a true New Orleanian will react as if the newly sober person has lost a dear loved one, or their sanity. And being a good Catholic will usually offer condolences, money, food, or even perhaps just one more cocktail to help them feel better. There are times I am a good drunk, last night I was a very bad one.

Once I sat at my stool, the one I always sit at, third one in from the door, on the short side of the "L" shaped bar, facing the inside of the room, door to the left, chosen deliberately so that I can see all of the women that come in, and thereby disregard the ones I have hit on or slept with already, Little Jimmy, the only other person at the bar more often than Miss Kate herself and who of course at 5 feet 9 and well over 300 pounds, left the descriptive "little" at the door when he was still in elementary school, slid my first drink in front of me without needing a word between us. I paid him, cash. There are no tabs, no checks, no credit or debit cards accepted at Miss Kate's, ever, and in my change Jimmy, as is his custom, included two bucks worth of quarters so that I could play the juke box. I walked over to the box and started to flip the sleeves that contain the songs, ten songs per sleeve and twenty sleeves in the box. It was while absently staring at the songs in the box, that the first real feelings started to stir inside, not so much loss, though the loss of her was and is still quite present, but more of a sense of how unjust the world can be. There, looking at the songs of Dave Bartholomew, Mac Rebbaneck and Irma Thomas I began to slowly feel the seething self-hatred that fuels the misery that is so much a part of the "nice" guy that everyone else seems to see and hear. A Hyde of self destruction that follows the Jekyll that is the sap that solves everyone else's problems, the idiot that gives so much of himself gladly to helping all of the others who are too weak to face their own meaningless lives on their own two feet. Yes, there, while I punched in the songs of my soundtrack of malaise and bitterness, I realized that God, indeed once and for all, screwed me, but good. And the only way to get God out of my head, the only way to stop the voices that scream "Face it, the wife beatin', lyin' loser mother fucker was better than you..." was to get so blind stinkin' drunk that I couldn't hear them any more if I wanted to. So I did.

But as I lay here on this rainy morning that the haunting images of what was did not leave. Instead, because they are burned into my brain, they glow brighter, until finally engulfing me in a conflagration of the past that scorches every fiber of my self, and now leaving me gasping and reaching for a sense of safety that does not exist. I start to think back. To the beginning of the end of me as a civil, sensible, free thinking, individual, and the beginning of the possession of my soul by a woman who no more thinks of me than she does of the man who creeps by in the dark hours of the morning to empty her cans of the other garbage she has tossed away.

Two

---◆━◆━◆---

CONTRARY TO POPULAR American urban myths sold by "life" coaches, spiritual gurus and self-help programs, I firmly believe we human beings actually have very little control over the path we take in life. Some of the twists and turns we encounter along the way we do indeed choose, others (and to me it seems the vast majority), are simply put before us, by whatever force you choose to designate. My own life path placed me squarely in the middle of nowhere as I delayed the onset of adulthood by firmly ensconcing my self in eight years worth of college. What can I say? I had an affinity for sitting in the "quad", smoking cigarettes and taking exams. After finally obtaining a degree in psychology, I floated through miscellaneous jobs in New Orleans until a friend told me that an advertising agency on Rampart Street on the edge of the Quarter needed an office go-fer. The job stuck, I didn't hate it and through years of good work eventually I left to take my first job as creative director at the New Orleans office of a small national agency, Bernard, Davis, Dossant and Evans. But, and whether or not this course chose me or I it, I was going through my divorce, and had become quite sick and tired of my life as it was. One Friday morning, about six months into the job, I got up from my desk, put a letter of resignation in a sealed envelope on my boss' desk and walked out of the doors. When she asked where I was going, I told the receptionist that I was headed out for a while. It was the truth.

While attempting to live a bohemian existence of minimal wants and necessities, spending my days reading Tolstoy and Walker Percy, making small change and getting stomped on by mad as hatter Arabian horses as a stable boy for a large horse farm just outside of my college town of Thibodaux, Louisiana; I realized that I indeed enjoyed the nicer things in life. So when the offer came from another large agency, J.Thomas Hunt, I jumped at the chance to again rid the American people of their hard earned dollars by convincing them that our clients had what everyone needs, regardless of what that was, from dish soaps to dick hardeners. Money is a great catalyst for reconciling oneself to the notion of work and though my job is not the most glorious or charitable of vocations, what the hell, I'm good at it and if somebody has to bilk the masses out of their meager earnings, it might as well be me. Besides, I get paid well for my efforts. And so it was that I left the stables and the beautiful Cajun countryside of Lafourche Parish Louisiana and returned home to New Orleans. But death-tight grasp of the most beautiful woman I have ever met in my life.

It was a Wednesday early this past January, as bitter cold and blustery as New Orleans can be in the depths of its short, but persistent winter, when I entered into the St. Charles Avenue offices of J. Thomas Hunt. Will Grace, the head of this particular branch was locked behind his office door with his secretary Bernadette (indeed the same woman who would end up delivering "the news" to me on the porch nine months later) in a Clintonesque dance that I would come to understand as the source of numerous bawdy titters that flew through the office first thing in the morning. I wandered about, found my office and immediately informed everyone I could find that I wanted to meet with the them in order to access the damage done by the recently departed former creative director. I was about to address what I thought was the entire staff, (Will and Bernadette emerged from his office shortly after I arrived), when Jessica blew in through the closed conference room door like a gulf storm. She was tall, and thin, particularly for me, as I tend to prefer big, full women who maintain their bodies and their presence in a similar fashion and consisted of all arms and legs and a mass of red hair that couldn't be tamed with whip and chair. She was dressed more for an afternoon bar crawl through the French Quarter than as a representative of several national brands (specializing in food), a virally infectious smile that she herself could not suppress and therefore no one around her could suppress theirs either, and she had those eyes. Big, ghostly blue and constantly agitated to a state of excitement so as to lead those around her, whether they knew her or not, to fully expect great blue lasers to leap from them, burning eye-sized holes into anything and everything in their paths, which they did, including and especially, me. The feeling at that moment, upon seeing her for the very first time, was that of willful submission of my entire self to her, whether she wanted it or not. Not bad for the first couple of minutes.

Three

——◆•••◆——

I HAVE TO stop this "remembering" crap or I will never get out of bed. Regardless of my dread, regardless of the weather, regardless of my ever-blossoming hangover, it is Saturday, and that means a forced march drive across the seventeen-mile twin span bridges, over the turbid and murky brown Lake Ponchartrain, to the bedroom suburb of Bentwood. A forlorn hamlet of outdated single story 60's and 70's ranch houses, strip malls, convenience stores and super-sized one stop enormo-retailers, that serves as a glorified rest area for transient families always looking for the next best place to raise two point three kids, a dog, and receive communal support and understanding after an admitted affair by one or both of the spouses with one or both neighbors. It is Saturday and that means Bentwood, Louisiana and grocery shopping for my elderly parents.

I shower, for as long as the hot water lasts, then while still wet and standing as close as I can to my Sears and Roebuck Kool Komfort window unit, I dress in my customary white crew neck t-shirt, light cotton long sleeve white button down shirt and then my frayed and faded Khaki pants that is the required uniform for New Orleans from May until October. I step cautiously out into the humidity of the late morning look into the forlorn azaleas and as expected see my paper, tangled in the bushes and mocking me from the mud with the stray garbage blown from around the neighborhood during the brief storm.

It is now late September and though that mythical creature known as

Autumn has begun to emerge from its hiding place in other areas of the
country, it is still clearly full on summer here. The rain has ended as abruptly
as it had begun, the hallmark of the monsoon rains in the tropics, where
moisture falls as if expelled from a great faucet, with thrust and force and
meaning, as opposed to places like the Finger Lakes region of New York and
in the northwest around Seattle, where the rain falls soft and unthreatening
but continues through days on end, in what seems like an endless gray misty
Ring Cycle, torturing the locals until bringing them to the point of wanting
to commit indiscriminant violence.

I stand on the porch and look about the empty street, the heat rising in a
ghostly soft vapor from the asphalt. I try to take a deep breath, but the air in
New Orleans from late spring until the first cool spell of the city's late coming
fall has an amazing thickness to it, giving it weight and volume and a presence
not known in the drier regions of the country. Here, the air is as much a part
of the local eco-system as its earth-bound cousins; the river, canals, bayous
and lakes. During the summer one breathes the air in whole chunks, so much
so it becomes another food group.

I am sweating profusely by the time it takes me to manage the twenty
or so yards from the porch to my car and as soon as I climb in I immediately
seek the refuge of the car's air-conditioning, but am forced instead to endure
my severely pre-owned German steam room and its ensuing blast of hot air
from the vents as the compressor loses the fight to cool things off. I think I
am going to throw up from the heat, or drown from the water pouring from
my forehead but gradually, as the temperature eases down from what has to
be the mid two hundreds, I find the strength to put the car into gear.

Before making the trek across the lake to my parents', I have a stop
or two to make so instead of going right to the interstate, I head first to
Tchoupatoulas Street, which runs to and from downtown along the river.
Tchoupatoulas is bordered on one side by the massive levee that keeps the
Mississippi in it's place, and derelict houses and stevedore companies on the
other. To my right, the river side, I see the very tops of the massive container
ships that have arrived from all over the world and wait at the various wharves
to be either loaded or unloaded. Slowly the street veers away from the river as
I drive under the two bridges that cross the Mississippi to the "west bank", a
bit of misnomer because though it is the west side of the river, as a result of the
unique geography of the city, it is in the same direction as the early morning
sunrise. I cut across the Quarter on Decatur Street, veering right at the island-
shaped French Market, with its countless vendors bustling about as they set up
their fruit stalls and second-hand junk to sell at the flea market. I have heard
the French Quarter described as everything from an adult Disneyland to a
shit hole that ranks only slightly higher on some mythical list than Tijuana

for taste and style. To be honest, being a native I never really thought of it as either, it's just "da Quarters", the place for once a year elementary school field trips and muffalettas from Central Grocery. My one great memory of the French Quarter was as a nine or ten year old and watching the final police raids to clean up the last remaining vestiges of "Storyville", New Orleans' infamous red light district, as part of the urban renewal programs of the early '70's. Today, the French Quarter, while less seedy, is instead rife with drop-out Emo kids from the suburbs, t-shirt shops and fake Voo-doo hustlers. All of whom bilk tourists for their money, and that's just fine with me.

Once past the French Market I turn left onto Elysian Fields Avenue and head "up" from the French Quarter, towards the lake and the tired suburban neighborhood of Gentilly, and my ultimate destination…Cosimo's Bakery. Cosimo's makes the best poor boy sandwiches in New Orleans and, therefore, the best sandwiches in the whole world. Mother is such a fan of Cosimo's fried shrimp sandwich, that it is required of me to bring one each time I visit. I am certain that after having made the trip to Bentwood almost every Saturday and holiday since my parents moved there during the height of white flight almost twenty years ago, it is in fact the sandwich she anticipates the arrival of, and not me. Even in Mother's current state of living, non-living, brought on by her own personal protest of life, she manages to wolf down every bite of a foot long shrimp poor boy, dressed with lettuce, tomato of course, extra pickles and mayonnaise. Proving to me that awareness among the elderly can indeed be a self-imposed, selective state.

Tiny white clamshells dredged at great ecological expense from the lake cover the parking lot that surrounds the two story, rundown, clapboard and wood-rot shanty that is Cosimo's. The restaurant (though in the thirty years or so that my family has been coming here, I have to admit that I never considered it as such) occupies the first floor; Cosimo and his family the three bedroom apartment on the second. The parking lot is full to the brim, as is the inside, with the Saturday lunch crowd, which consists, not surprisingly since Cosimo's is well off the beaten path that the tourists generally tread, of hard-core locals and quite a few New Orleans police officers. I park near the back of the building next to one of the blue and white patrol cars, emblazoned with the city shield and the moniker "To Serve and Protect" on the side. As I open the door to get out of my car I am assaulted again by the heat and humidity, which, when combined with the great amount of alcohol still swirling in my system, causes me to actually feel the blood flush from my face as if some unknown being has just pulled the chain. My knees give and as I desperately reach for the front bumper of my car, I begin, with a great heave, to throw up every inch of what appears to me to be my large intestines, all over a discarded bag of Zapp's "Craw-Tater" Potato Chips and a half drunk strawberry ICEE. Not wanting to focus on my current pathetic situation as I puke, I instead think of the commercials for ICEEs from when I was a kid and hear the voice over announcer calling out the drink's slogan that ICEE is "The C-c-c-c-coldest drink in town". I wipe my mouth with a partially used napkin I find wedged under the front tire of my car, look at myself in the passenger side view mirror of the cop car and see that the episode has caused the blood vessels above and below my eyes to burst, giving me the look of having the crap beaten out of me, which in essence I have. I gather myself and slowly sliding my right foot ahead I feel for the first step, the left slides behind the right until I finally gain momentum and stumble to the front of the building and a well-deserved lunch.

As I walk through the dark green painted glass front door, the frigid air-conditioning flash-freezes my sweat covered body and the remaining alcohol from last night seeks every opportunity and every pore to escape. Cosimo's looks like any of a thousand po-boy shops in the city. Roughly 15 terrazzo-topped tables are spread randomly about the restaurant, with cops occupying about half in two groups. The sandwich counter runs the length of the room from front to back on the left side, forming a salad and meat-filled barrier between the kitchen in the back and the glass walled front. Upright drink coolers line the back wall, half with soda, half with beer. To the right sits Mister Jerry, manning the register. As I walk in, from behind the counter a booming voice which can only belong to Rudy Cosimo, calls out loud enough for everyone to turn in my direction,

"Man, you look like shit…again. What is this, the second time this week you've done this to yourself?"

"Third, but who the hell is counting…except you of course." My whole body hurts when I speak.

"You ever considered actually taking care of yourself?"

The smell of the deep frying food wafting from the kitchen causes me to fight the last of my rising intestines and for a dreadful moment I worry that I may lose the battle again right here on the cops, but I manage to stifle the urge, "Why bother?" is all I can say as I reach for the stability of the counter to lean on and rest my burning forehead on the cool glass front that displays the different meats and salads. Cosimo's potato salad is my favorite, though looking at it now in my present condition; lumpy, egg yellow with crusty peaks at the corners causes second and third thoughts.

"Pick your head up for God's sake." Cosimo's voice sounds like a cannon, he turns to the kitchen and calls,

"Hey Willie, come check your boy Hanson out! He lost a fight with da bottle again last night." Willie, the elderly black man that has worked at

Cosimo's since Mister Jerry opened the original place a couple of doors down in 1964, walks over to assess my rapidly worsening condition.

"Damn Mister Johnny, dis da wurst I ever seen you." He pauses putting a hand on my shoulder. "I seen this many, many times Rudy and I'm tellin' you only a woman could do this to a man, ain't dat right Mister Johnny, it's dat woman from your office, that one you brung in here a while ago. She done this to you ain't she?"

"Not today Willie" I stammer back at him. I want to climb into the cooler with the salads, if only I could lay down for a few more hours, not much, just a week or two.

"Willie, the garbage in the back is full again" Rudy's wife Margie calls from the back room.

"I'm gettin' to it Margie!" Willie, still standing next to me yells back to her and magically cleaves my head in two using no more than his voice. "Damn sad…" is all he says shaking his head as he walks to empty the cans.

I feel something cold and wet hit me on top of my head and seeing it hit the floor in front of me barely recognize it as a pickle slice. I look up to see Cosimo smiling, "You awake? I'm makin' the sandwiches for your mom and dad…can you eat and if you can, what do you want?" he asks as he pointedly slathers mayonnaise on my mom's fried shrimp sandwich. I fight my big intestines back into place again, or maybe it's the small intestines this time, "Roast beef, dressed, fries…I gotta go sit down"

"For here?" Rudy doesn't even look up as he grabs a new loaf of French bread from the pile at the end of the counter and slices it into thirds.

"No, I'll take it with me, if I eat it now it'll just be a rental"

"Gotcha, go get a Dixie Beer, that'll help" Rudy takes the bottom half of a 14 inch piece of French Bread and reaching into a steaming pan of roast beef and gravy, with a large spoon, scoops up gravy and spreads it onto the bread. Then grabs a set of tongs, picks up large hunks of the meat and covers the gravy. His motion is fluid and ritualistic and done while turning to greet other people who walked in after me and damn them, obviously feel better than I do.

I make my way along the drink coolers, stop long enough to grab a Dixie long neck, stumble over to the counter that holds the cash register, where Mister Jerry sits on an old barstool reading the Times-Picayune's Sports Section and waits quietly for someone to argue sports or politics with him. I use both hands to open the beer with the ancient Coca-Cola bottle opener that is screwed into the counter, and I fall into a chair at a table nearest to the air-conditioner just before I would have collapsed into a cotton, khaki and sweat heap onto to the floor. The beer cools my throat, which rages from the effects of stomach acid hurtling out of me at near light speed on its way to the ground, I raise the bottle to my forehead where its curative effects on the fire that seers my forehead rivals the touch of the Lord himself. The sandwiches are ready in minutes; I go back to the counter and collect them from Rudy, and feeling the pleasant buzz that comes from the marriage of old alcohol and new in the bloodstream, decide to grab two more beers for my drive across the lake. I pay Mister Jerry without a word about the current black administration, the Saints or "the Federalists" as he calls the national government, and hurry to my car, imagining my invalid mother desperately wheeling herself back and forth in front of the living room window that looks out onto the parking lot of their apartment complex wondering where in the hell her sandwich is.

The drive from Gentilly to the twin span bridges on Interstate 10 takes me through New Orleans East, essentially the largest middle class slum in the world, filled to the rafters with substandard housing and apartments built by mostly scam contractors in the late 1970's and 1980's on land barely reclaimed from the swamp as they built. The whole of the area is already falling down around the largely poor and middle class black population that, thanks to the current housing boom, can't afford to live anywhere else. Beyond New Orleans East on the border between Orleans and St. Bernard Parish, I pass a derelict amusement park that stands as a stark reminder of yet another failed city government's attempt to create something out of nothing. Don't get me wrong, there are a lot of great things about this city, my city, but as the state, federal and local governments all line up to fail the residents, the good and great of the city tend to remain contained within the limits of the city as they were defined prior to the end of the Second World War. Nearly everything added to New Orleans in the 60 years since then has flourished briefly, then left to rot.

I finally I hit the twin causeway bridges that span this end of the massive lake, the car cruising happily at near ninety, and two cold beers for company, I open one of the beers and allow myself to drift back two months, to earlier in the Summer, when everything changed for me, from how I work, to how I look at the world, to how I love, or more appropriately now, refuse to love. Whatever the case may be.

Four

PEOPLE FIND THEIR own way of coping when confronted with the most wretched and mundane task, especially when they discover some beneficial external reason for performing that task that has nothing what so ever to do with the task itself. For instance, I have a buddy, Mike, who worked as a mailman for a while before attending college. He absolutely hated the job. His supervisor was lazy and indignant, especially, when, in an effort to put Michael in his place as the new guy, he gave him, as Mike describes it, the "shit" route. The longest, toughest carrier route they had in Algiers, Louisiana, a hamlet of old shotgun houses similar to my rental located just across the river from downtown New Orleans. Michael's supervisor, who he described as an embittered longtime postal worker who probably never saw "A Miracle on 34th Street" and how the post office bailed Santa out of a tight spot, confronted Michael before he went out on the route the first time he was going out and told him that it would be late that evening when he finished, if he was able to finish it at all.

Now Mike is like almost every other native New Orleanian, he'll do just what he needs to do to get through the day, do it well, and he'll do it in his own good time, unless of course, you tell him he can't do it. Then a streak of determination a yard wide shoots up his back and burns so hot in his head you can literally see the smoke come out of his ears. In Mike's case he took the mail and walked out of the Algiers Central Office as if he were going out for a nice afternoon stroll, got into his car (they didn't have enough official postal vehicles back then) and drove to the neighborhood. Once there, he took his mailbag out of the back of his car, and started running. He ran the whole route, blocks and blocks like some demented mailman version of Forrest Gump. He says to this day he has no idea how long the route was, but all the mail got to where it needed to go, all the mail that needed to be picked up got picked up, and he finished the whole route in just three hours. When he got back to the central dispatch, Michael's supervisor was so pissed at him he made him work the rest of his shift in the sorting room instead of allowing him to go home early. After that, Michael, having learned his lesson, went out on his route and still got the letters out as quickly as possible, but to make sure he didn't have to sort mail any more, he flirted with, and screwed as many of the women on his route as possible, sometimes two or three in a day. So, in spite of the fact that Michael hated his job, he adjusted so that he was still able to show up every day and do the work.

I don't really like advertising. It is a meaningless occupation in an increasingly meaningless world. I often need a good excuse to show up in the morning, but usually settle for boredom and money. After only a week at J. Thomas Hunt, I was back on familiar ground and hating what I did for a living. Advertisers prey on the weak, the fearful and those whose lives are in **such** bad straits that their low self-esteem is actually the only bright spot in an otherwise pathetically dismal existence.

"Do your feet hurt? Here, try Dr. Bunyon's guaranteed orthopedic supports. What's the guarantee? You'll pay forty bucks for 90 cents of foam and plastic."

"Can't get a hard on, or want one to last all day to help that office fantasy seem like an absurd reality? Then you need Perm-R-Ect by Franklin Pharmaceuticals"

"Wife left you, dog left you and you want to make yourself feel better? Then you really need the brand new FORD Everest, the biggest fucking car in the world. It's so big and so fuel in-efficient it comes with its own tanker truck. The upside is it is so big, it will even help you get past your small dick complex".

There are days when I should take my shower after work instead of before.

My upside, my reason for doing the job, was that Jess was there. Every day, nine to five, or reasonably close, except on Wednesdays when her baby-sitter had to leave early for night school. On those days Jess had to leave by four fifteen to pick up her daughter Amalee from the after-care program at her Catholic school. From that first day that I saw Jess in the office, she was my inspiration, she was the reason I got out of bed in the morning, the reason I put up with Will's demeaning and condescending attitude towards everyone who wasn't under the desk blowing him. Jess was the reason that, dangling as I was on the career cliffs, ready to concede my soul to the sponsored rocks below, I was able to find purchase with my fingers alone and hold on. Go to work? Hell, I was early! I wanted to be there when she breezed or rather bullied her way through the door in the morning. She moved not so much with grace, but with a determination to reach her destination. Every corner of every desk, every edge of every wall from the front door to her office was a barrier to her progress, often seeming to come alive and jump out into her path: it was as if she had to fight the very forces of nature to find her desk and turn her computer on and begin the day. For beautiful as she is, smart as she is, creative as she is, Jess is not a morning person, not even remotely, and she struck back at the morning as if she were fighting some unseen, but vigorous, assailant, and I made sure to show up every day to watch the battle. Because even then, red hair flying about her as if each strand were trying to flee in a different direction, face bare of the make-up she didn't need anyway, her pre-noon scowl firmly affixed, and her mouth uttering syllables more closely resembling some ancient dead language than English, I was already madly in love with her. I placed her on all of the campaigns that would require the biggest share of my attention. For two reasons: one, she is an immensely creative and talented person. And two, I wanted any excuse I could think of to spend time with her.

And so, we did. Great mounds of time, often whole days with each other as we took meaningless campaigns from concept, through the production of the commercial, the editing and finally airing on the various channels, either local or national, depending on the client. During my first few months there, we were work partners, then as we spent more time together our discussions outside of the work world drifted to talk of our families, our marriages, our divorces, how we succeeded in our relationships and how we failed. She told me of her daughter, of the love they share, and how together they manage to get through so much that had happened to both of them when her and her husband broke up. I told her of the miscarriage my wife had in her fourth month, at least, I said, I assumed it was a miscarriage. Jess and I became acquaintances, then friends. I grew to respect her, both as a co-worker, and also as a person. To understand her as the person she is, helped along by the rugged individuality that she possesses, the sense that she is who she is unapologetically, a rare and beautiful gift, especially in this day and age of mass conformity.

One glorious Thursday, a little less than six months to the day since I arrived at J. Thomas Hunt, Jess asked me if I wanted to get a drink after work. I was stunned, I actually think I went brain dead for a moment or two as the words rattled around inside my head like loose bolts in a great tin pail, until they finally deposited in the right receptacle and I was able to communicate a barely intelligible, but ardent "Yes". It was the end of June, the twenty-ninth to be precise, we had both worked late on the same project with one of the editors, and after seeing him off, we walked the two blocks down St. Charles to the Ponchartrain Hotel. There sitting in the elegant mahogany bar, drinks in hand we conversed like two normal people out for a drink after work. It was amazing. We managed to stay for more than just one, Jess being a native New Orleanian like myself; her drinking prowess is not hampered by size, stature or sex. She tends to enjoy shots, bourbon of course…she is no slouch when it comes to drinking. When it was time for her to leave, we walked back to the office and to our cars. She pulled her keys out of her back pocket and unlocked the driver's side door which I opened for her and, completely consumed in the moment, we reached for each other and kissed, not the quick kiss on the cheek of the co-worker, but the long deep kiss of lovers long held apart but still forced to encircle each other at close proximity. We kissed so that all thought, all knowledge, all sense and sensibility was taken from us and we became the kiss itself. Hearts beating, pulses racing, heat rising between us until we met inside of each other. It was a damn good kiss.

I drift back from that moment to the driving in time to see that I am finally getting across I-10's twin bridges into St. Tammany Parish, the border of white trash civilization marked by a giant billboard advertising "The Bead and Trinket Mardi Gras Warehouse", lovely. I finish the last of the beer I got at Cosimo's, and leave the lake, the city and her far behind me. As I drive I feel the phantom pain of her pressing against me once again. I sit here now, four months and what seems like an eternity later, and realize that I will feel that goddamn kiss for the rest of my life.

Five

My MOTHER IS indeed waiting for me; I look up at my parents' window while still in the car and see her looking back, one hand holding the faded white curtains apart, the other letting a half filled coffee cup slouch forward. I am waiting for a car in front of me to pull out of the parking space I want, an end spot near their apartment. Though my car is far from new, I still want to lessen the risk of some redneck in an old Dodge pick-up pounding into one of my doors as he fumbles with the grocery bag full of Pabst Blue Ribbon beer that he saved up for all week, just so that he could drink them while watching more rednecks circle a track surrounded by a hundred thousand more rednecks drinking more Pabst Blue Ribbon. A southern version of one of the seven circles of Dante's hell. The car finally backs out; I pull in and shut my engine off. I pause for a moment to take a deep breath, then gather up the sandwiches as well as my courage and get out of the car.

As I open my parent's door I see that Mother has wheeled from the window to the small entryway of the apartment, effectively cutting me off in an effort to confront rather than greet me as I walk in.

"It's about time" she spits.

She looks as she does every day, tired and drawn, her face lizard dry and wrinkled, her hair that was once kept shoulder length and reminiscent of Donna Reed from the 50's television show is now matted, skimpy and gray. Her arms, mostly covered by the three quarter sleeves of the housecoat are dotted with large dark spots and bruises from her insulin shots and from

23

bumping into cabinets and table edges in her wheel chair. She insists on forgoing the clothes in her closet, in order to spend her days in her housecoat and pajamas. My father has become quite diligent with doing the wash since taking over the household chores, especially since he couldn't find the laundry room in their house for the first thirty years they were married, yet mother's housecoat is still covered with stains, mostly from coffee, but she does have the odd food stain here and there. On her left shoulder she appears to have suffered a recent ketchup spill.

I look beyond my mother's wheelchair barrier and see my father. He has thinned a lot in the last few years to a shadow of himself and is no longer the infinitely strong and athletic man I knew as a child, thanks in no small part to the ravages of alcohol, cigarettes and taking care of Mother. We looked alike before he lost the weight. The "me" I see in him now terrifies me, because I see my own long slow fade. He sits glued to his beloved Chicago Cubs on the television and ignores Mother's cackling. Not that he needs the game for distraction, because though his time is largely spent caring for Mother, my father has learned the blessed ability to completely shut her voice out, a character trait that I rank second only to being able to perform miracles. He leans toward the television to watch as a player for the Cubs has "just driven the ball to right". The television volume is set to "deafening", and I sense the whole apartment building can hear 39,000 rabid Cub fans scream in unison.

"They'll lose" Mother screams, "They're bigger losers than the Saints."

My parents both turn 80 later this year and have been married for almost 60 years, and through careful observation conducted over the length of my own forty years of association, I am certain that my mother, while she may have loved my father, in her own way, has never really liked him, a subtle, but important distinction. My brother and I, coming as late to them as we did, were needless to say, not planned pregnancies. As I got older and began to notice who my parents really were or at least who they appeared to be to me, I found it hard to believe that these two people were ever either emotionally or physically close enough to actually have sex. As I grew into manhood or some form thereof, and experienced for myself the hunger of sex and the desire of another person to share my time with, I began to think of my parents as automatons, emotionless shells of whoever they may have been but are no more.

"You just had to park in that one spot didn't you. I saw you waiting for almost ten minutes for that nigger from downstairs to leave. There were at least five empty spaces out there. I took my insulin shot a while ago you know."

"It was not ten minutes Mother, and can you try not to say something completely offensive soon as I walk into the house?" I lean over to kiss her cheek and mock her shitty demeanor by being saccharine sweet, "How are you doing? Did you get out of your wheel chair today?"

"Why the hell would I want to do that and exactly how am I offending you?" she says as she grabs the bag of sandwiches from my hand, places it into her lap, and wheels into the kitchen.

"Hey Dad…how you doin'?" I call out to my dad as he stands, his hands jingling the change in his pockets. He reaches for his shirt pocket as he starts to move, obviously the Cub half of the inning is over and he's going to the back deck to smoke.

"Hey, John, I'm going out onto the back deck to have a cigarette, you wanna join me?"

"Sure let me help Mother with lunch first."

I walk around the short wall that separates my parents' entry hall from the small eat-in kitchen to see that my mother has already dumped the contents of the bag onto the small oak table and has scooted two of the old ladder backed kitchen chairs to the side so that she can sit directly at the table in her wheel chair. She has tuned everything out as she unwraps the white butcher's paper from her sandwich. I stare at her while she does this and for all I know it could be the buzz from the newly resurgent alcohol in my blood stream, but I can swear I see saliva dripping from the corner of her mouth.

"Mother, are you drooling?"

"Itsth my new lower plate, from that fucking Yankee dentisth" She spews the words out as she shoves one end of the shrimp poor boy into her mouth.

"You going to eat?"

"I think I'll join Dad for a cigarette first."

"Suit yourself. Can you get me a diet Barq's out of the fridge before you go outside?"

I get my mother her root beer and leave her contentedly devouring the sandwich; the sound of her lips smacking together follows me out of the kitchen. I walk across the apartment and in crossing it in only a few steps, am struck once again by the small size of it. I can never understand how any two people; especially these two; manage in such a small space. In inflated housing boom/bubble real estate jargon it would be known as "quaint"; in real words it's called a cell. My parents, throughout the entire time of my childhood and until I left for college, lived in two large houses in New Orleans. The first, a mid-sixties two story in a subdivision called "Lake View" and located across Elysian Fields Avenue from what was then known as Louisiana State University in New Orleans, but is now just the University of New Orleans. It was my favorite; it's where my friends were, where I could just go out and play and where I fell in love for the first time. The second house, was much larger, and because of its location in the uptown section of the city, was much more "dignified" as my mother used to say. They didn't have to move, they didn't want to move, the second house was just a house; bought to placate my dad's need to move, for no reason in particular. My parents lived well, "lived" being the operative word. Because now they don't live at all, they "get by", whatever the hell that means. Though my guess is that now, in the last stage of their life, when they ought to be, at least, trying to enjoy living off of everything my father worked some fifty odd years to earn; first as an appliance salesman then assistant store manager, then store manager, then rising through the corporate ranks to retire as a Vice President for the now defunct D.H. Holmes retail chain, instead of living on all of that, they "get by" on social security and veteran's benefits while jammed into a slapped together shit-hole second story apartment, on the outskirts of a town where everything, including the million dollar mansions at the country club, is a slapped together shit hole.

The one redeeming quality about the apartment, for my father at least, is the unobstructed, almost bird's-eye view of the twelfth tee of the Royal Palm Municipal Golf Course. Number twelve is a bitch of a par four for even good golfers at four hundred and seventy yards. It has a slight dog-leg right and rows of plumb straight forty-foot high evergreens lining the tight fairway. As I slide the slightly grimy glass door open, condensation from the air-conditioning runs down the length of the glass leaving long streaks, taking two or three years of filth with it. "Thwack", a short fat man wearing gold LSU shorts and a red shirt that has become a deep maroon thanks to thirty or forty gallons of sweat has just teed off.

"Ha!" my dad blurts, "He'll need a goddamn Indian guide to find that one!" He takes a drag on his cigarette and I notice that he is holding a drink in his right hand, vodka and tonic.

"Jeez Dad, they'll hear you."

"Ha!", he says again indignantly. I want to go back inside, but would rather take my chances with my father getting into a shouting match with fat golfers than sitting inside the apartment alone with my mother until he comes back in. But it's a tough call. We have many inherent differences, my father and I. For instance, I prefer to go through life unnoticed; I don't send food back at restaurants, am not an activist for any cause, I don't speak at city council meetings or help someone in distress. Hence no one can form an opinion of me, good or bad. My father could give a damn what anybody thinks, especially after he's been drinking. I watch him closely as he, with a swift, smooth rhythm, takes a sip then a drag of his cigarette, never taking his eyes off of the foursome as the next guy, same build, same sweat as the last one, brothers, maybe cousins, maybe both, considering we are north of the lake and civilization, tees his ball up.

"Besides they can't hear me down there." He says as he offers me a Viceroy, I take one and he lights it. I exhale a plume of smoke as Whack! "Fat Guy Part Deaux" wallops a low, line drive that screams up the fairway before hard slicing and hitting one of the evergreens along the right side of the fairway like a cruise missile. Thock! The ball ricochets off of the trunk of the tree and shoots back out into the fairway, albeit only a hundred or so yards from the tee. The second fat man cannot believe his good fortune and razzes the first fat guy; it's obviously a money game.

"Member's bounce there!" my father yells to the foursome, the first fat guy flips my father the bird with the hand that is wearing a black Foot Joy golf glove, holding it high above his head like a short fat white parody of the two American sprinters from the '68 Olympics.

"Asshole!" my father yells back as he turns towards the sliding glass door where he pauses, drains the last of his drink, takes a last drag and then flicks his cigarette in disgust towards the departing foursome, "Let's go eat" my dad chuckles. I toss my cigarette over the railing of the balcony and into the neighbor's yard as we head inside. The combination of the cigarette and oppressive heat has re-introduced waves of nausea and I feel the need to eat and then lay down.

My mother is just finishing her sandwich as we re-enter the cool air conditioning of the apartment. "Yelling at the golfers again?" as she jams the last of her sandwich in her mouth. This is one of those days where my confusion over whether or not my mother hates my father is cleared up with the first words I hear between them.

"Not yelling...commenting, Mother."

"You're just mad that you can't play any more." She wipes crumbs of French bread from her mouth with the back of one hand as she backs her wheel chair from the table with the other, "I don't miss it." My father says as he walks past the liquor cabinet eyeing the enormous 2 liter plastic bottle of cheap vodka that sits on the top.

"Oh...no, you don't do you? You'd much rather be stuck in here lifting me onto and off of the plastic portable fucking toilet and watching me sleep." Mother is wheeling towards us as we walk to the kitchen, the tight space forces my father and I to back away as she rolls past us to the faded green Sears and Roebuck corduroy chair that she spends her days in. My father watches her and sighs, almost but not quite inaudibly, then continues into the kitchen.

"What did you get for me?" he asks ignoring my mother's last remark.

"Panned Veal dressed, with mayonnaise", although when I say it, it sounds like "Mah-nez".

(Pronounced pah-nade, with the long "a" sound in New Orleans, it is veal or chicken that has been drenched in an egg bath, dredged in bread crumbs or corn meal and then pan fried)

"You sound like one of the illiterate natives" my mother shouts back, still sitting in her wheelchair. She has the remote control, and is flipping through the channels so fast there's no way she can know what's on. My head is spinning.

"I am one of the illiterate natives. Mother, do you need help getting into your chair?"

"I'm fine"

"Are you sure?"

"Yesssss." She says. She is already annoyed, which is her natural state.

"Just leave her alone John" my father quips as he sits at the table, having just poured himself a Diet Coke.

"You want something to drink?"

"Yeah, Pop, a Barq's would be great."

My mother tries to lift herself from her wheelchair into her armchair. No easy task as she has gained some fifty or so pounds from her usual 125 that she weighed when she cared about herself, others and life. Her weight ballooning in the last few years largely thanks to her self-imposed confinement to a wheelchair which began shortly after my brother's death. She grunts as she pushes herself up, steadying herself with her hands, her forearms arms pressing into the wheelchair for support. She strains so hard she passes gas as she lifts herself. She manages to stand briefly, then collapses into the Sears chair with a thud. Clearly this is as much physical activity as she will get today. I stare and for a moment think back to my childhood and to the mother I grew up with, the mother that was, as is traditional in Southern families, the centerpiece of the family. This in spite of the fact that she was a transplant, having spent the first thirty years of her life in her and father's native Indiana before his job moved them south to New Orleans in the late fifties. My father has kept some of his Midwest traits, mostly his pessimistic attitude, fondness for bland food and passive-aggressiveness. When you speak to my mother and ask of her origins she makes it a point to ignore Indiana and will only speak of extended ties to the south through her mother's family in Greenville, Mississippi. She plays the southern card whenever she can and perpetuates stereotypes by being defiantly bigoted, preferring to rationalize it as most southern whites do by referring to what they see as an obvious difference between "black people" and "niggers". "Black people" are industrious, hard working and educated. "Niggers" are shiftless, government funded, pregnant, un-educated and when they do work it's as drug dealers or gangster rap artists. Bigoted Southern whites like Mother believe it's okay to create these distinctions because whites are burdened with the Jerry Springer white trash and there is little difference between them and niggers. In other words, Black People, we feel your pain.

My parents tried for years to have kids. My mother would get pregnant, then as happened some four or five times, she miscarried before the fifth month. Finally, in 1961, at the age of thirty-six, she carried full term, most of it in bed, and gave birth to my older brother Harry. Four years later, she got pregnant again; this time she carried easily for nine months and yours truly was the result, a strapping nine pound seven ounce blob of joy and happiness. To Harry and I mother seemed to flourish as we got older. She was involved in the PTA, she car-pooled to school and baseball and football practices. Because she was older than the other moms in the neighborhood and was the product of Depression she was the only mother on the block to bake her own cookies, cakes, and brownies, all from scratch. Harry and I were mortified of course; we would plead with her to buy cookies from the store to no avail. When she was in the kitchen, all the kids in the neighborhood managed to find their way to our back yard just as something was coming out of the oven to cool. They of course thought it was great that our mother actually used the oven for something more than cooking frozen pizza and Thanksgiving turkey.

In the winter of 1990, right before his thirtieth birthday, my brother Harry began dropping weight for no reason at all; he just lost his appetite the way a person loses their wallet. He became sallow and listless, and was constantly thirsty. Finally, almost reluctantly, my mother took him to the Oschner Clinic for tests. Harry was diagnosed with type 2 diabetes. My mother, expecting the outcome, nevertheless was crushed, for you see, twenty years earlier, on a bright New Orleans fall Saturday, as she was upstairs making our beds, Mother collapsed onto the floor and two days later, she was diagnosed as diabetic. Mother would always say that she had "given" my older brother her disease, it was a bond that would define their relationship from then on, a holy union that excluded both my father and I, and neither he nor I would forgive either of them.

"You gonna eat your fries?"

"Only a few dad, help yourself." Despite the beer wearing off, the sandwich had me feeling much better. Behind us in the living room, my mother, let out a low snore. "She's down for the count." My dad says not bothering to look over to her, still munching on his veal sandwich, "It's pretty much all she can do to stay awake long enough to eat, you know she can't even make it all the way through 'As the World Turns' anymore."

I get up and walk over to my mother. She sits in her chair head back, mouth open, I look at the remote control for the television held in her right hand and think to myself that she has a "death grip" on it, either the morbidity or the humor or both makes me smile as I wrestle the remote out of her hand.

"What should we do about grocery shopping?" I ask my dad, as Mother turns her head and shoulders slightly and snores louder. I wish to myself that she would close her mouth.

"I'll go on and 'make groceries', you look like you could use a nap too, stay here with Mother, we don't need much, I won't be long." My father, despite his mid-western upbringing loves using New Orleans' slang every chance he gets, like "making groceries" for grocery shopping. Every Saturday he and I dance this same dance and I always insist on going, if for no other reason than to get out of the apartment, but today I'm too tired to dispute him.

"Okay, but let me give you money."

"No, John." My dad refuses me half-heartedly, he needs the money and he knows that I know that, damn his politeness. "Here Pop," I say taking out my wallet and handing him five twenties, "I would've paid for the groceries had I gone." My father takes the money, "Thanks Johnny," he grabs his keys from the bar, "stretch out, I'll call on the way back so you can meet me downstairs."

"Okay dad, be careful."

"You too, she's even more feisty when she wakes up from her afternoon nap."

"I'll keep my hands away from the bars."

My dad laughs as he walks to the door. He won't say it out loud, but I know he is glad for the time alone, he and mom spent little time together before she got to be like this. With the way things are between them now, I'm always a little surprised when I get here on Saturday and see that they aren't both lying on the floor with their hands around each other's throat; too weak to actually kill each other they merely lie on the ground, in each other's clutches until I show up, pry them apart and give them lunch.

Lying on my parents' rumpled and off-color white sofa I flip through the channels until I find what I am looking for the soothing sounds of Bob Ross, talking of using colors like sienna and burnt umber to create "happy" fall trees along the shore of his make believe lake. I think of this past summer, and of taking Jess to meet my friends Tim and Andy at their Fourth of July party. Tired beyond belief and feeling lost to the alcohol and a full stomach I close my eyes.

Six

———•◦•◦•———

I LOST MY virginity at thirteen to the older sister of a kid who played on my 13-15 year old baseball team. She was seventeen and thought that I was fifteen since I had been practicing with the fifteen-year-old all-star team, when in reality I was just a good thirteen-year-old that the coach thought should get the chance to play with the bigger kids. He had no idea of the chance that he would really be giving me. Her name was Laurie, that much about her I remember. The evening it went down had all the ingredients needed for teenage sex; an FM radio tuned to WRNO and Captain Mellow, the coolest DJ in New Orleans at the time, Miller Ponies, those tiny little Miller Beers that came in seven ounce glass bottles, and horny kids. When Laurie and I left the others at the impromptu party in the third floor observation deck of a local apartment complex, I thought we were just going for a walk to talk, about what I had no idea because outside of baseball, I really couldn't communicate about much, especially with girls. So I was fairly surprised when she abruptly ducked behind a row of thick hedges, jerked me into the bushes after her and found a space large enough for the rolling and fumbling that I gradually, even in my youthful naiveté, grew to recognize as my first sexual encounter. It was, as they say, over before it had begun and looking back, I seem to remember having the same feeling as I did as I first looked at the always large number of presents Harry and I received for Christmas, sort of a mixture of wonder and mystery, with an appropriate amount of gratefulness sprinkled in.

As I have mentioned already, I have been married once, for four years to be exact, though to be really exact, three years eleven months and thirteen days. That was six years ago. I've had one girlfriend in the meantime, not counting Jess, (but then again I can't really count her, it's the whole exception to the rule sort of thing), for two years beginning immediately following the collapse of my marriage. That relationship ended the day I walk out of BDDE and into a horse stable, and she felt I probably wouldn't be able to keep her in the lifestyle to which she had grown accustomed. I have slept with somewhere in the neighborhood of a hundred or so different women, of all shapes sizes and colors, but please, don't tell Mother. From the time I was thirteen until now, and through all of it, all of the lying, all of the hurt caused by and to me, through all of the games played by both sexes in order to gain a foothold on the loneliness and self doubt that rules who we are and how we act towards each other, I think I might have been truly in love exactly one time, and Jess was it.

Maybe.

I do remember that as soon as we finished that first kiss after work, and she put her car in gear and drove away, I knew I felt something. We talked to each other on our cell phones exactly three minutes later during the drive to our respective places, hung up as we parked, then called again once more to say goodnight. She seemed to be as happy as I was that this had happened, at least I hoped she was. I hoped that I wasn't going to be hung out there alone, in that dreadful space where a moment occurs between two people and one of the two thinks that the moment is pure magic while the other finds the moment to rank somewhere between "really nice" and the same level of excitement they feel when they get the oil changed in their car.

I hung up with her and laid in bed wide-eyed and tried to figure out to the second how long it would be before we saw each other the next morning. I forced my eyes to close and replayed the whole evening front to back and in rewind. I still heard her, saw her, smelled her and wished to God she were still with me. The next day we both tried to act as if nothing had changed, as if we were just two people working together. I would find any excuse to go down the hall to where her office was just so I could look in, maybe say 'hey' and then skip back to my little corner of the world. Finally, after rationalizing my sixteenth or seventeenth reason to go into her office, I crept down the hall, we snuck a kiss and parted like grade school kids, giggling and flirting.

It's not like I don't know what love was; I found that out in third grade. I couldn't express it, but I had an idea that love was what was burning inside of me every time I got to Mrs. Caluda's class and saw Marcia Barrios walk through the door. Every time my hands would sweat when I would look outside of my window at McDonough 39 elementary school, see the rain coming down in buckets onto St. Roch Street, and just know that we would stay inside for gym, which meant square dancing, which meant that I would actually get to hold Marcia's hand as we danced the Virginia Reel. That was love. Pure love, real love, Gene Kelly singing in the goddamn rain love, not yet tainted by the lust for a girl's/woman's body that would blossom after my roll in the bushes with the misguided teenaged baseball groupie, and that would ultimately ruin everything I touched, like Midas gone mad. I had no idea how much I had become tainted with the stench of modern love, if that's what you call it, until that evening with Jess, when she magically transported me back, body and soul to the simple kid who thought that world began and ended with one person's touch.

Our first kiss at the end of June meant that the July Fourth holiday was fast approaching. My friends Tim and Andy had invited me over to their house on the Mississippi coast with fifty or so others for their annual Fourth of July Party and Drag Show. Invitations for the event are hard to come by, but they are old and dear friends and former co-workers from my days at BDDE, so I've been to the extravaganza every year since the first. I called to inform them of the recent change in my social situation and they enthusiastically told me to bring Jess. I hung up with Tim, and walked/ran down the hall to her office and quietly asked, she accepted and our first chance to have a real date was set.

For me, the Fourth couldn't come soon enough. I got exactly seventeen minutes sleep over the two days immediately prior to the holiday, thanks to Will volunteering to move a deadline up in order to appease a client even though he didn't have to do the actual work. I worked until the afternoon on July Third and when it looked like I wasn't going to finish and the day was nearing the seven thirty drop dead time for overnight shipping, Bernadette happened to walk past the edit room with Will close behind her. He stepped into the suite, looked over our shoulders, saw where we were or rather where we weren't and began hinting to the editor and I that we may have to come in the next day on the Fourth to finish. We waited patiently until Will walked out of the room and I turned to my editor, a pleasant earnest fellow affectionately known as Aussie Bob and said,

"Bullshit".

Thankfully Bob wanted to get out of work for the long weekend as badly as I did and so in a brilliant act of co-conspiracy and with a couple of quick keystrokes, he trashed the editing computer we were working on. Trashed to the extent that after a phone call or two to tech support and with Will back in the room to witness, it was determined that an expert would actually have to come in to the office and perform an onsite internal drive scan or some other such technical crap. I didn't know and I didn't care, the main thing was that it wouldn't be possible for anyone to come to perform such technical crap until at least the seventh or eighth. Screw Will, that'll teach him to volunteer me for shit without asking first. Aussie Bob poked around for a few minutes to make it look good and we were both out of the door before Will knew what hit him. The last words I heard as I literally ran out of the door were the ones Will stammered over the phone to the client as he made up an excuse.

Thankfully the Fourth landed on a Monday, because Tim and Andy's party was taking place at their weekend house on that Saturday and two days would be just enough time for me to recover. The house is a lovely six bedroom Cyprus retreat built in the early 1930's for a prominent New Orleans family, who used it occasionally during the hot pre-air-conditioning summers to cool off, hide the booze that they bootlegged into the city during Prohibition and plot against Huey Long. While some of the guests would begin arriving as early as the day before, the real festivities wouldn't begin until the afternoon of the Second, I told Jess I would swing by around noon to pick her up. Mother had the nerve to actually call me that morning and ask me if Jess and I could drop off lunch to her on our way to the party. Knowing that the rare pleasure of introducing Jess to Mother would end anything between she and I before having a chance to get it started I did the only thing I could and lied. I told her I felt bad and decided to stay in the city. Mother actually tried to press me into coming over, but finally retreated after I told her that I could, but didn't think I could manage to stop for her sandwich. Screw her.

On the morning of the party I was dressed, sitting and sweating in the car by ten. After going back inside for a second shower, a change of clothes, changing clothes again, changing clothes a fourth time, resigning myself to the fact that I'm an oaf, turning the TV on, flipping channels, turning the TV off, walking through each of the rooms of my house, walking in and out of my patio door, looking in the mirror again, and calling myself an oaf again, it was finally time to leave to pick Jess up.

Jess lives in a carefully restored 1920's cedar plank shotgun house in the Mid-City section of New Orleans, a beautiful area away from the river up Canal Street from downtown. The avenues are draped in ancient oaks that prove their strength by forcing their roots up through the sidewalks and streets. The houses are mostly modest like Jess', broken by the odd block of larger double portico houses, so named because of the second floor balcony that is situated above the first floor porch and, less often, by some sort of brick and aluminum creature spat out in a hurry during the sixties or seventies.

I had to drive past my old high school to get to Jess' place and as I turned off of Jeff Davis Avenue on to Webster Street, where she lives, my mind flashed back to that faithful day in 1980 when, on that very same corner my high school girlfriend Maureen Regan waited for me one crisp fall afternoon. I walked out of the building clad head to toe in the khaki uniform required by the local Catholic schools and saw her sitting quietly in her Datsun. Maureen was infinitely more mature than me and proved it by having a job out in Metairie at Lakeside Mall. She owned the Datsun, bought and paid for it herself and, because she didn't trust me behind the wheel, did most of the driving. I got in, and leaned over the stick shift to kiss her, at which time she promptly turned away. I couldn't imagine what I had done in that short amount of time to piss her off. We hadn't talked all day, in fact she had just come from school herself and was still dressed in her school skirt; solid brown and hemmed at the knees for propriety. She also wore one of those great Catholic school girl, pretty-much-see-through, short sleeve blouses, which highlighted her bra and in turn, her great seventeen year old breasts. Looking back I wonder how the hell did anybody expect us **not** to have sex. She must have known what I was thinking because she jammed her foot sharply on the accelerator and we took off down Webster Street. As I stared at the football team as they climbed into buses for the trip to City Park for practice, she started crying and proceeded to tell me she was late. I said she was right on time and that I was the late one, having just finished with my math tutor, as algebra always gave me fits. At which point she proceeded to call me an ignorant asshole and said that she wasn't talking about time of day late, but about her body, she was late for her period. Then she said she was like clockwork and never late for her period. Finally, she let loose a great explosion of tears that she had evidently been holding back all day. Unable to drive, Maureen pulled the car over near the end of Canal Street in front of the Odd Fellow's Rest Cemetery and continued crying, black tears from her mascara streaked her face and dropped to her white shirt, where of course they landed on her breasts. I sat in stunned silence, tried not to look at her chest and instead looked at her stomach and wondered what it would be like to be an eighteen-year-old baseball playing dad. She wanted to know what I was going to do about it. I said that I wanted to have a chance to think about it considering she'd had some time with it; even then I was not one to make impetuous decisions. She said that's pretty much what she expected me to say, she called me an asshole again and told me to get out of the car. I got out, she drove away and I walked back down Canal to the Carrollton Avenue bus, sat by the window and noticed every baby on the planet for the next two days, when, as luck would have it, Maureen got her period. She asked me to forgive her, I did, and she tormented me for the rest of my senior year, sitting behind home plate at my baseball games and ridiculing every pitch in every game until my sports psychologist told me to get rid of her...which I did.

Twenty-four years later and about a hundred yards from where my ride with Maureen began, I found Jess' house after a couple of passes up and down the street and pulled into the drive at exactly eleven fifty-nine and fifty-five seconds. I shut the engine off as I rolled to a stop, something I immediately regretted when the largely irrational terror struck me that the goddamn thing might not start back up. As I sat in the car cursing out loud, I saw the front door open and then the screen door. Jess stepped out onto the porch and she was beautiful. She was dressed casually for the heat, and completely out of character. She wore a pair of white linen Capri pants and sleeveless plaid blouse. Her hair had finally been tamed and forced into a ponytail and she had even gone so far as to even have an aqua blue Kate Spade shoulder bag slung over her left arm. After seeing her dressed in a variety of clothes for work, including the occasional pair of camouflage pants and combat boots given to her by her brother, a former army officer who served in the first Gulf War, it was nothing short of astonishing to watch her walk to the car looking for all the world like a soccer mom on her way to meet the girls at Starbucks. I caught myself staring with my mouth open before I jumped out of the car and ran around the back in time to meet her at the door. Thankfully she waited for me to open it; I hate it when women open car doors for themselves.

"You look…" I started,

"Don't say a word." She interrupted,

"But…" I stuttered. She talked as she slid into the car,

"My mother came by to pick up Amalee because I couldn't get my asshole ex-husband on the phone and it's supposed to be his weekend with her. She dressed me."

"Who, Amalee?" I said, leaning on the car, not wanting to move, and hoping she hadn't notice the sweat that had formed on my upper lip and forehead.

"No you jackass, my mother. You getting in?"

"Oh. Yeah."

As I ran around the back of the car again, giddy as a madman, I prayed to God Almighty that my heap would start again and then continue to blow cold air. I plopped down into the car and watched her as sweat beaded on my forehead. My stomach hurt, I was nervous as hell and couldn't figure out why. With no clear cut answer I decided to chide myself again for being an oaf, a big fat sweaty middle aged one at that. She lit a cigarette, and interrupted my self flagellation by talking to me.

"We'd probably get to the party sooner with you driving us rather than loitering around in my driveway." She took a long drag.

"You think so?" I said as I started up the coughing and wheezing old kraut.

" Yeah I do. Besides, I'm starting to sweat."

She caressed sarcasm like a lover, and eased it into conversation whenever she could. I backed out onto Webster Street and noticed that though I have driven through this neighborhood a thousand times since getting my license at fifteen, being with Jess that day made it seem to take on all new dimensions. I had to stop in the middle of the street before putting the car into first gear. I took a breath and re-oriented myself. The air conditioner belched old dust in a cloud from the middle vents, part of an ancient dried oak leaf fell to the floor, and then magically, cold air began to come out again. I caught myself looking at her.

"What's wrong?" she asked.

"Not one thing," I said as I turned my head away, I told myself that I had to stop looking over at her or I was going to run into something and kill us both. Neither of us talked at first, instead, she smoked while staring out of the window and I drove. Geographically between two people, it is an odd place to find yourself when you begin a relationship with someone that you've already known on a certain level. Having begun things with Jess as a co-worker, then, inexplicably we moved to another place, another more personal place and seemingly without any time to prepare. I felt like I knew so much and yet so very little about her. And I also felt that this drive ahead of us that was somewhere in the neighborhood of ninety minutes, was going to fall on either side of some invisible fence. One side where we could become intimate and revealing, where we would begin to learn the things about each other that we would use to build a true relationship. Or the other side, the dark and cold side where we would soon learn that spending five minutes alone with each other was a form of hell that cannot be replicated without conjuring Satan's minions to dance in the backseat. It is that type of hell that causes so many first dates to be emotional exploratory surgery in the form of a drink or two in a very public place. Propelled by a morbid sense of fear by one or both that they don't want to be trapped in anything as claustrophobic as a full dinner with no planned escape route. It's because of that fear that many people today have become aficionados in the art of the thirty-minute date. Deftly dismembering the person they are with mentally down to their smallest neurosis, and tossing the bad ones back like an undersized fish.

"I can't tell you how nice this is", she said as she eased the seat back, slid her feet out of her sandals, then hiked her legs up and rested her feet on the dash. She rolled the window down a little to let her smoke out. I wanted to light up so bad I could taste it but new love had me trying to quit. She took another drag and let the smoke out easily, "Every day is the same, I work my ass off, then come home to take care of Amalee. I haven't been on a date in I don't know how long."

"Is that what this is?"

"Yeah, in a way."

"In a what way?"

"I mean yeah it is a date kind of, but it isn't because I don't know if I am ready to date yet."

"We can call this whatever you want, or we can not call it anything and just have a good time."

She turned to me and gave me that great imperfect smile that she has that is at once both sexy and incredibly goofy,

"I like that, I could use a good time."

"Well then, there you have it."

As far as I was concerned she could call this shit on a stick, as long as we were together, it really didn't matter to me. After we got the labeling out of the way we fell into our own separate silence again, not a bad silence though, more like we were okay with it. In spite of the lack of traffic, I kept to my routine for city driving and cut through the neighborhood side streets on my way to the interstate. Unlike other cities, newer cities mostly, where clear economic boundaries exist to mark the separation of rich and poor, in New Orleans people of all monies, "the Haves and the Have-not's" as Huey Long used to call them, share many of the same streets and in some cases the same blocks. As we drove further from Mid-City and closer to the interstate and downtown, there was no question as to where the poor of New Orleans live. Cheap and rusted barbeque grills lined with aluminum foil formed the hub of the inner city 4th of July gatherings that had started to take place on the small swatches of brown, patchy and untended St. Augustine grass that makes up the median or "neutral ground" between the lanes of avenue traffic. With Lake Ponchartrain so polluted it has long been unusable by residents, fire hydrants sprayed water and plastic pools dragged to the neutral ground from the back yard were crowded with swarms of black kids who were and are so screwed by the crappy Orleans Parish public education system, that probably half of them couldn't tell you why the Fourth of July is a holiday in the first place. Black men, most of whom are so squelched in life by an ancient caste system that they have no real future and no real past, tended the fires loaded with cheap cuts of meat, while large women in halter tops and shorts sat on coolers and lawn chairs and drank. As I finally got to the on-ramp for the interstate, the city began to depress me so much that I couldn't bear my thoughts any longer. I looked to Jess who was staring out of the window.

"So what were your mom and Amalee going to do today?"

"They'll probably spend the day at the club."

"What club?"

"My parents belong to Sweet Briar Country Club."

"Get out of here, ya'll belong to Sweet Briar?"

"Yeah," she continued to look out of the window, "those barbeques we passed smelled good." I couldn't tell if she was trying to change the topic. I was curious because Sweet Briar is the swankiest of the swank and the weekend home to the golf, tennis and bridge games of the social elite. Growing up solidly middle class, there was no way my parents could afford to join, even if they had been asked, but having attended the premier boys Catholic school in the city, and been a baseball star to boot, I was invited to my share of sweet sixteen parties, debutante presentations and any other excuse for the cream to show the rest of us how much higher on the class pole they were. Sweet Briar meant money for sure. Jess kept talking, and still looked away.

"I don't go to the club myself, the people there kind of creep me out. But my folks still do, my dad sits on the board since my great-granddad was one of the founders."

"Pardon me...One of the founders? And what, may I ask did your great-grandfather happen to do for an occupation when he was out founding Sweat Briar?"

She twitched in her seat, and looked a bit uncomfortable; I began to feel that I had asked too much.

"He was the president of Great American Steel at the time." She mentioned this as if it were a burden.

"He was what?"

"He was president of..."

I interrupted "I was kidding...you know...for effect. I actually heard you the first time. So your Great Grandfather..."

"Maris"

"Holy shit. As in Maris Shipping, with the big boats, international offices in London and Hong Kong as well as the twenty something story building downtown?"

A visibly pained expression appeared on her face,

"Yeah."

"I can't believe all this time and I didn't make the connection. I'm a fucking idiot.

"Maris is my maiden name."

"Is your name on one of the..."

"Yeah, one of the super tankers that daddy leases to Exxon/Mobile is the Jessica Louise Maris"

"Oh, just one of the super tankers that daddy leases...okay..."

"But I don't really care about the money or anything, you saw where I live, I'm not rich."

"Hell, you got to be rich just to talk like that."

"No, I really don't, I mean it was always there and I know that, don't get me wrong. But beginning with high school I've wanted to be on my own, to get my own job outside of the family, make my own money, buy my own house and live my own life and I have, much to the dismay of my mother."

We were cruising on the interstate by now, lifted above and bisecting the city as the I-10 cut its way right through the middle. The day was incredibly hot, and with the air conditioning working better than I had ever hoped it would, I could still feel the heat as it rose from the concrete and surrounded the car.

"Were you a rebel as a kid?" I looked over at her, and she appeared to be as cool and composed as if she were on a Sunday drive in the family Bentley, the heat probably had to ask her permission before it bothered her. Again I felt suddenly inadequate.

"I didn't see it as rebelling, I still don't. I'm just trying to make my own way, my own name, there are so many expectations when you grow up in a family like mine, I just said 'fuck it' and decided to do what I want. Though…" She paused, I could see in her eyes she that she was weighing her next statement, trying to decide how much she wanted to say, trying to figure out what I would do with the information.

"Marrying Stephen was I guess a way of rebelling, a really stupid way."

We were now going over the high-rise bridge that spans the Industrial Canal, where I worked on the docks as a stevedore for my uncle in the summer breaks from college. The canal bisects the city, with New Orleans on one side and the Lower Ninth Ward, one of the city's first suburbs and for the last 20 years or so a mostly black neighborhood on the other. The Lower Ninth is poor by even New Orleans standards, and that means it's also violent…even by New Orleans standards. New Orleans cops don't so much patrol the Lower Ninth as contain it.

"So why did you marry him?"

"Why did **you** get married?" After driving through most of the city looking away, she finally turned to face me, and showed me that she directed the retort as I took it, as a Tit for Tat. Fine, I was up for it.

"I got married because I was almost thirty and living with my then girlfriend and had already been to therapy with her and figured that getting married was what we should do."

"You had already been to therapy together, before you were married?" She laughed.

"Yeah, pretty fucked up right? But to me, and I guess to her it seemed normal, natural, you know? Every body who is married is in therapy or should be, I just figured we were ahead of the game."

"Did it help?"

"We were together for five years, in therapy most of the time and in the end she ran off with the therapist. Not the one we started with, I don't even remember that one. We had something like four or five different therapists over the five years. But all things being equal, I think…no…I know that we are both better for the whole deal. So in the long run, yeah I think it helped, if for nothing else it helped us realize how much we didn't like each other."

I looked at the speedometer and saw that I was pushing near ninety as we shot past the area known as New Orleans East. I realized that being with Jess even as we talked about something as pathetic as my marriage, removed the depression I normally felt when I passed the run down apartments and the deserted amusement park.

"That's good…I guess…isn't it?" she said as she reached to the dash and scratched the bottom of her foot.

"What's good?" I was lost in her, lost in the ride and also lost with what we were talking about.

"The therapy helping you realize that you didn't like it other, that's good isn't it?"

"Yeah…" I say drawing it out unenthusiastically.

She lit up another cigarette and cracked the window again to let out the smoke and officially let in the heat again. My back started to perspire and thereby also began sticking to the seat. I thought of Martin Short and a character he played back in the days when Saturday Night Live was funny. Short was an obvious crook, being interviewed by Harry Shearer, who was portraying Mike Wallace from Sixty Minutes. He chained smoked and sweated profusely as he tried to lie his way through the interview, his lies as obvious as the river of sweat on his upper lip. I caught myself mid-thought, and became worried that she'd think that I'm something of a wide-eyed narcoleptic. I jumped back into the conversation so loudly that I scared her.

"You know, I should've had an idea that things perhaps weren't as good as I thought they were, or maybe that they were as good as they were going to get when she walked into the bedroom one night, we had only been married…I don't know, a year and a half, maybe two. Anyway, she had just finished getting ready in the bathroom, brushed her teeth, whatever, and she climbed into the bed. I was re-reading, "Lancelot" by Walker Percy…the thought of us having sex was out of the question because from almost the beginning of the actual marriage we had sex only a couple of times a month. So anyway, she climbed into bed and then as if she had been hit by some sudden revelation, turned to me and told me that everything she had fallen in love with me for, she couldn't stand any more."

"Ouch, that's hard."

"You know, I didn't realize how hard a statement it was until after we broke up."

"Really?"

"Yeah, I think when she said it, I kind of laughed, not thinking she really meant it, that maybe she was kidding, but looking back after we broke up, I can see that she wasn't kidding."

"I married Stephen to piss off my parents"

"Did it work?"

"Oh hell yeah...like a charm."

"Did you love him?"

"Positively, and to be honest there's a big part of me that still does, even though I know I can't trust him, and I know that he doesn't really care and I know that it is, in the end a very bad situation for me."

(I want to interject here and say that had I not been such an idiot I would've seen the big red flag that popped up after she said that last sentence. But no, that would've been too rational, and since when is love or lust rational?)

"What do you love about him?"

"I love that he's bad, that he's like 'Fuck you' to everybody in ways I can't be. Until of course, he was like 'Fuck you' to me. But still..."

She looked out at the passing white caps that rolled on top of the lake, the winds that created the chop were off of the Gulf and had the look of a coming storm, maybe not that day, but given the conditions and the length of time since the last one, we were certainly due.

We were almost across the causeway by now, not quite three quarters of the way to the party. Apparently we were going to be okay spending time together.

"He went to jail right?" I was curious about what I had heard about Stephen around the office, but as soon as the words were out I felt like I had failed miserably in my attempt to bring it up delicately.

"Yeah."

"For what?"

"He got busted selling some pot, not a lot, but enough for a few months in Orleans Parish Prison."

"You stayed with him through all that?"

"Hell yeah, you think my parents were pissed when we were dating? You should have seen them when I would go to visit him in jail, they couldn't even speak to me, and I loved it. We got engaged while he was inside."

"Nice. Romantic...in an 'Escape From Alcatraz' sort of way."

"Not really, I was already pregnant."

"Oh."

I began to think that this was the point in our conversation when it would have been a good time for it to get quiet between us again. I mean what could I say to that? I may not be the coolest most hip guy on the planet, and I understand that in certain circles, doing time is a great way to build credibility among your "peeps", but all things being equal, I'd rather win an award or pull someone from the burning hulk of what is left of their car or eat the most hotdogs at Nathan's Coney Island. Because, and call me wacky, spending twenty-three of twenty-four hours of each day in an eight by five cell for any length of time is not my idea of building my resume'. I was locked in a holding cell once when I was in college in Thibodaux, for the heinous offense of driving with an expired license. Shit, I even knew the cop who locked me up because he worked the door of the club I managed. I was locked up for only a couple of hours. Mostly because my girlfriend was taking her Microbiology final and she would have to drive my car home. When I walked out of the small town, Barney Fife of a jail that I had been in, to look at me you would have thought that I was Nelson Mandela for God's sake. I bent down and kissed the ground and swore to God and my unborn children that I would never enter a jail again unless it was to deliver Christmas baskets and soap on a rope.

"I went to see him every day I could." Jess went on, "It was humiliating, going there, getting searched by the guards…"

"Searched how?"

"Really searched inside and out. The women guards would rub me down, check me over, it was sad, pathetic even, but I was in love and I felt bad for him, even though he had done an incredibly dumb thing to get put in there. I couldn't help it."

I sat there dumbfounded as the mobile home dealers, strip clubs and truck stops of Bentwood flashed by.

This guy, this complete fuck-up of a guy had broken the law, something beyond the realm of my understanding. He had willfully committed an act that would allow someone to take him away from this amazing woman. What the hell was he thinking? I became immediately jealous that she had gone through all of that just to visit him in jail. Hell, I've dated women that wouldn't visit me in the hospital if I were lying unconscious and covered in bandages from pulling the aforementioned people from the aforementioned burning hulk of a car. Unless the hospital were offering a buffet lunch and 2 for 1 on bar brand liquors and bottled beer. After my divorce I had become convinced that I had no concept of what love is and Jess' statement of blind devotion to this guy proved it.

"So how did it end for you guys?" I tried to sound unaffected by my new found hate for this guy.

"Amalee was about to turn two, she and I were in the living room, I had just gotten my job at J.Thomas Hunt, everything was so new still between us as a married couple. He had been out of jail for a little while and was working pretty steady, a rarity for him. And then…he began to go out on his own at night more and more often. But I didn't ask any questions, I never did, I just felt that as long as he came home everything was alright."

"That's kind of a thin line."

"Yeah thanks for telling me."

The sarcasm dripped from her the way the sweat dripped from me. She lit another cigarette, drew on it deeply and stared at the Mississippi countryside and seemed to have gotten lost in the evergreens that flashed by, standing quietly at attention like the earthen Chinese soldiers in an emperor's tomb.

"One day Stephen walked into the house from work and told me he had to talk to me, something he never did. So I sat down on the couch and he sat in a winged back chair that neither of us sat in and he told me he was in love with another woman, that they had been seeing each other for a month, and that he wanted a divorce and he was going to marry her as soon as he could."

"Holy shit."

"Stephen wasn't one for beating around the bush."

I watched her smoke her cigarette down to the filter and couldn't take it any longer.

"Can I have one of yours?" I said as I pointed to the pack that sat between us on the console. She picked up the cigarettes, opened the lid of the box and slid one out with the skill of a repeat offender.

"I thought you quit." She smiled as she said the words.

"So did I." I said as I put the cigarette in my mouth, swept up the lighter, created flame and sucked in every ounce of the tar and nicotine. I rolled my window down and immensely satisfied, blew some of the 3000 or so carcinogens into the fresh Mississippi air.

"I'm really sorry about what happened to you."

"Why, you didn't do anything."

"I know, but still. He and I are both men and…"

"And that's where the similarity ends, so let's leave it at that."

So I did, I left it at that. But her story hung suspended in the air with the cigarette smoke as we spent most of the next twenty minutes of the ride, the rest of the ride actually, in quiet. But not an uncomfortable quiet, more like a respectful rest for what we had both been through trying to love in our lives.

Seven

———◆◆◆———

"MOTHER!"

My dad's voice jolts me out of my sleep and I instinctively sit upright on the couch, I turn around as I was sleeping facing the back of the couch, to see my mother laying on the floor at the foot of her Sears chair. My father drops the bags of groceries he's carrying and sprints across the room, moving faster than I have seen him in years and falls to the floor trying to wake her, but she is not stirring. "Don't just sit on your ass Johnny, call 911!" He yells at me as he leans over to see if she is breathing. I jump from the couch, my head hurting so bad I feel that someone is following me turning the screws on a great unseen vice that is attached to both temples. I hurry over to my parents' phone, which sits on the kitchen counter next to an old notepad with my brother's last employer, Mason Pharmaceuticals, written across the top. Not counting of course, his quality employment after he really got enthusiastic about his drug use, which included part time stints at convenient stores and a warehouse worker for the Salvation Army. Looking at the pad I notice the top page still carries all of my brother's numbers even though he has been dead for five years. I sigh and slowly dial 9-1-1 and while I wait for someone pick up, I thumb through the other pages and soon realize that though every pharmacy, liquor store and social service in Bentwood is written down as well as a couple of third and fourth cousins, none of my phone numbers, past or present are anywhere to be found. I try not to become angry at my unconscious mother who lies just a few feet away from me, but find it difficult.

45

"What's that ma'am?" I say to the operator, trying to focus on the job at hand.

"Where are you calling from?"

"2311 Dogwood Lane Apartment 2A", I watch Mother, looking for that tell-tale last breath, the operator interrupts again.

"Is your mother breathing?"

"What?"

"Is your mother breathing sir?"

"Is Mother breathing?" I call out to my father, thinking that if she is, she's probably lying there thinking about my brother.

"Yes!" my father calls out, "Where the hell are they? Have they left the goddamn firehouse yet?"

"The ambulance is on the way." Evidently the operator heard every word.

I suppress the urge to tell them to take the long way.

"They should be there in approximately three minutes." She says coolly.

"Great, thanks."

I hang up and walk back over to my father who holds Mother's left hand with his right and has his left hand on her forehead slowly caressing her. I wonder if the compassion he is showing is genuine or more of a reflex act, the product of nearly sixty years of 'Yes, Mother…of course Mother…right now Mother', I was always fascinated by the fact that he never, ever called her by her first name, only 'Mother', but then again, that was all I ever called her as well.

"What the hell happened, didn't you hear her?"

"No, I really didn't, I was sleeping." I look back towards the kitchen and thinking of the leftover sandwiches, suddenly find myself hungry for some reason; maybe I should grab a bite if we're…

"You were passed out, I smelled your breath when you got here."

What the hell is that?

My father, he of the afternoon toddies, he of the car rolling backwards down the driveway into the neighbor's front yard because he was so drunk and had to piss so bad he put it in neutral instead of park in his hurry to get inside?…he of the fucking shots of bourbon chased by Falstaff beer after his Saturday round of golf? People who don't know him well think my father had a stroke when they see that his right hand is closed into a perpetual grip, but you hold a highball glass every day for two or three hours over the span of sixty years and let's see you straighten your fingers out.

"I was nor passed out, just sleeping"

"I called the house phone, I called your cell phone, you were too drunk to answer, you were passed out, don't argue with me"

Where the hell is that ambulance? I do not want to go down this road with my father, I do not want to say something I'll…

"I hear the siren." He says, looking toward the front door.

"I do too."

My dad leans down to my mother, he puts his lips up to her ear, "It won't be long now honey, I know you can hear me, I know you know I'm here, you're not alone, you're going to be okay." I must have some sort of expression of disbelief on my face as my father looks disapprovingly at me as he finishes lying to her. He disapproves of my reaction? At least I'm honest. He's the one who should be ashamed of himself, especially when he has the nerve to call her 'honey'. What does he think? That maybe I haven't been around the two of them for forty years? *Wrong, boss, I was right here the whole time, you keep the charade going for everyone else out there, but I was right here.*

"She'll be okay."

"I hope so, I can't imagine being without her."

He can't imagine being without her? He's waited on her hand and foot for the five years since Harry died, he fed her, bathed her, lifted her off of the portable toilet that sits dead in the middle of the fucking living room and wiped her ass when she said she was too tired to reach her pathetic arms behind her. What can't he imagine being without? Even before, even when things were 'good' between them he treated the marriage as if it were something arranged by their parents.

My folks never hugged, never kissed, and certainly never said 'I love you', not to each other and certainly not to Harry and I. Not to me anyway, but she showed it to Harry. Because he was 'special' to my mother, when he died she sat in their living room and wailed "Oh, if only he had been loved!" Loved!? Harry went through two wives and scores of girlfriends before he decided to drop dead. "Loved!?" Hell. She loved him, more than she ever loved me, sorry, and maybe I'm an insensitive bastard, but I don't want to hear it.

I hear the paramedics stomp up the stairs, and I run to open the door for them. I try to back out of the way as they pull the stretcher through the open door and set it near my mother. My father stays with her as they lift her on the stretcher and reverse their process, banging the doorframe and awkwardly carrying her down the stairs. Her head lolls back and forth with the motion of the stretcher and she looks for all the world as if she is truly dead, but I knew otherwise, I knew she was just fine. My father makes a couple of attempts to get his foot up onto the bumper before finally climbing into the ambulance. He turns back to me after sitting down with a harsh exhalation on a metal emergency kit, "You follow us to the hospital, I'll ride with Mother."

I lean in and try to hear him over the calls of the paramedics and the subsequent radio chatter. "What hospital are you going to?" I shout, though he is only a couple of feet from me. He just looks back and shrugs. There were two or three large facilities where they could take Mother, Bentwood has no lack of places to take the ill, the injured or the addicted, in other words it is a typical American suburb, and besides the town has more than its share of the elderly who seemingly move there just to die.

The paramedics finish loading their gear, one guy walks to the driver's side as the other waits for my father to get settled and then pulls the doors closed behind them. As the ambulance pulls away I turn and finally notice that the neighbors have all come out to see what is going on. They line the edge of the parking lot, all of them jostling and pushing each other to see who can get the best view. Little kids, mostly black, but also a couple of white trash kids, all with their permanently dirt-smudged faces, hands and feet and wearing only shorts with no shirts, are running back and forth from the ambulance to where the grown-ups stand. The kids are playing some kind of game that involves touching the ambulance. I begin to feel queasy and wish to hell that they would stop because it reminds me of the mob scenes from the movie version of Tennessee Williams' "Suddenly Last Summer". I slowly drift into a black and white world of Katherine Hepburn and Montgomery Clift, but am brought right back to the Technicolor here and now by the cough of the ambulance as the driver starts the engine and turns on the siren. I think the siren and lights are more for the kids than to denote any kind of emergency as my mother's condition, while unknown, appears for the time being at least, stable, so I don't see that they would hurry. As the ambulance pulls away my father looks back at me and I, instead of waving or showing some sign that I think will reassure him, turn away uncomfortably and look around at the apartment complex with its ratted and chipping ply board doors, fading paint and unattached gutters and quietly curse my brother. For it was his addiction, his cunning and either their naiveté or their willingness, that pushed them out of the house that was supposed to be the place they'd spend their last years and led them here. I look around one last time as the noise of the siren begins to fade into the distance and I smile, realizing not at all unpleasantly, that I like feeling the hate that I have for my brother and walk to my car.

I am, in all earnestness following, though at some distance, the ambulance when halfway between my parents' place and the hospital I see a squat little red building called Two-Two's Steakhouse, complete with a large stuffed cow on the porch and a neon sign in the window that says "Dixie Beer" and decide to duck in for a quick one or two or four. Not knowing how long it will take to assess and admit my mother, I realize that last thing I really want to do is sit around the hospital without some kind of alcohol related buzz. I pull up and park next to the cow, which on closer inspection shows the respectable hole in the forehead made by one hell of a shotgun blast (slug, not shot) that's been loosely patched with what looks like old cat fur. As I'm getting out of the car my cell phone rings, I look for the caller ID and break into panic driven short breaths and forehead sweat as I recognize it as Jess' number. Torn between wanting desperately to talk to her and not wanting to talk to her I choose the latter, flip the phone closed and walk in. I am still in the throes of my miniature panic attack as I breech the coolness of the Two Two's air conditioning, make eye contact with the bear sized, middle-aged man behind the bar (who I learn is not "Two-Two" but his younger brother Harley) and sit at a stool between the draft handles and the drink rack. Behind me are four or five small tables and in the corner a Plexiglas table that consists of a Ms. Pac Man game that has to be at least twenty-five years old. The dining space beyond that is thirteen or fourteen tables, each covered by a vinyl tablecloth with a squat bulbous red candleholder in the center. The tables are surrounded by four chairs, sans cushions and all made of thick dark pine with a shiny lacquer stain that gives the place the look of having been furnished by a fan of early American Wal-Mart. Undoubtedly the food must be great. Harley is wiping down glasses in preparation for everyone of the fourteen or fifteen people that the bar area can hold comfortably at its maximum.

"What can I get you?" Harley bellows, using the bar towel over his shoulder to wipe the sweat off of his forehead. Before I can answer I hear the message chime on my phone go off. Knowing that Jess' voice lies somewhere in the circuitry of the phone is not unlike knowing that Poe's Pendulum sways just above, getting painfully closer with each pass.

"Shot of Jameson's and a beer",

Oddly enough, thoughts of my mother begin drifting away, especially after the first true warmth of the whiskey settles inside of me. At the same time however, the weight of my phone in my pocket begins to double, then triple, then increases by a hundred times as I can't help wondering what she has to say. The anger of unfairness rises as I order another shot and gulp down half of the beer, the second shot calms me as I wait for what the character Brick in "Cat on a Hot Tin Roof" called the "click"; that moment when the alcohol takes control, when it sits in the pilot seat and I am able to fasten the seat belt of un-reality and take off. My phone rings again, I tentatively take it out of my pocket, but this time it's my father, "Hey Dad…"

"Where the hell **are** you?" he yells so loudly that feedback reverberates from the earpiece of the cell.

"Where the hell are **you**?" I answer back a bit too lightly.

"Don't be a smart ass, they've brought her to North Lake Regional, you would know that if you had followed behind."

"I needed gas so I stopped and just held up figuring you would call when you got somewhere."

"Unh-hunh." My father knows that's not what happened simply because had he not ridden in the ambulance, he would have done exactly the same thing.

"Bring some beer and a Styrofoam cooler, we're going to be here for a while."

"Right Pop, I'll be there in a few minutes."

"Alright, it's not like she's going anywhere." My father sighs and hangs up; I can tell he needs a drink. "Shot of Jameson's" I call to Harley, who has wandered down to the other end of the bar to talk to an old woman with a walker who sits drinking a tall draft beer. I over hear their conversation, "Awww, the whole fucking system sucks balls" the old woman spits as she takes a last sip of her beer. Harley nods as he turns from her, grabs the whiskey and pours me another shot. I drink it, the third one slides down with hardly any after burn, the "click" is coming. I decide that it's finally time to listen to Jess' message as I pull my phone and my wallet out of my pockets.

"Hey John…I'm guessing you might have heard something kinda big… about me and Stephen…I just wanted to say…I don't know…he's different… changed. I don't know why it's important to tell you, it just is, I guess because in a lot of ways I still love you, but I have to try again with him…but I want to talk…I don't want to hurt you and I want you to know that you… "

I lose my signal and my phone dies in mid-sentence, but what is the fucking difference, "I love you, but need to be with him?" What the hell is that? What the hell could we possibly have to talk about? What is it about women that it's not bad enough that they tear your fucking heart out, but they have to do it again and again? I'm beginning to think that love for me is a bit like Quantum Mechanics, something I know to exist, but have no idea how it works.

I have to get beer for my dad and get over to the hospital, so I pay for my drinks, toss my phone in the garbage can behind the bar and walk out into the blinding and unforgiving sunlight of another crappy Louisiana Saturday afternoon to go see about my mother.

Eight

PEOPLE ARE ALWAYS amazed when something unexpected, and yet completely natural with the order of the universe occurs and turns their world around. Every once in a while a story will come on the news regarding a swimmer; man, woman or child, who is attacked by a shark off of the coast of Florida, and when interviewed for the national audience, those who saw the attack or knew the victim are genuinely surprised by the whole event. In spite of the fact that they, like the victim were frolicking around in the shark's house, looking for all the world like something the shark would want to eat, or at least taste. The shark was just being a shark, doing what he does, no more and no less. And yet, we aren't surprised when we ourselves bite into what ever it is swimming around on our own dinner plates.

People are also surprised when family, friends or acquaintances die suddenly. This is because they don't want to admit that life has death, that the two are inter-connected and as of now and in spite of what Ted Williams may or may not have believed before being frozen in carbonite or whatever, there is not any way to tear them apart.

People are also just as surprised when relationships end. This however isn't a result of not wanting to admit anything; people are surprised when relationships end because those same people are largely in denial about love in the first fucking place. The chief component of that denial is the admission that love has un-love, the place where love ends, like a path disappearing into the woods. Un-love is full of hurt and more often than not, full of anger. Hurt

51

at the loss of one presumed to be the life partner, the sharer of all things good and bad. Anger at the deception, intended or not, that this was the one. Anger at time lost following the McGuffin, the false trail…the dead end. For one out of every two marriages, love, if it ever existed at all, goes away after a couple of years, awash in a litigious stream of he said/she said. I was not in love when I got married, so when the marriage ended it was more of an inconvenience than a true painful experience. Perhaps that is why I was able to fall in love again. Because I hadn't gone through enough pain, if only my divorce had been truly hideous, I wouldn't have quite had enough of the requisite hope to get into another relationship. But I did.

That is why just three and a half months ago, the pain of un-love was the last thing from my mind as Jess and I drove past the tall thin sap filled evergreen trees lining the narrow state road in the hazy and dripping wet Mississippi July heat.

We were quiet, she absorbed in whatever she was absorbed in, which she disguised by looking at the trees going past and me, never one to miss an opportunity to check out for a while, I wandered away, to the safety of thinking about my senior retreat, held in a Carmelite center not too far from here, twenty plus years ago during the spring semester of my last year in Catholic education. The retreat was supposed to be three days of "reflection and prayer in hopes that God would have a forceful impact on our lives". What it was in reality was three days away from parents and coaches, three days of sneaking off into the deep woods to smoke pot and confide in our closest friends about our deepest fears and expectations of our coming college years. What I remember most of the retreat was sitting on a sap-sticky felled evergreen trunk out of eyesight of the main retreat building with five or six of my fellow soon to be grads when Jimbo Troslcair blurted out that he had gotten his girlfriend pregnant. We all just sat there looking at him. I remembered my own previously recounted run-in with the stork some two months earlier on the corner of Webster and Carrollton and thought to myself that considering Maureen had not been pregnant, and the way everyone got quiet, I was glad I had kept my mouth shut. I was glad I had kept my mouth shut. We all sat there in that silence knowing in our heart of hearts that we were lucky not to be in Jimmy's shoes. I would say that the most important decision for all of us coming out of that retreat was a firm belief in contraceptives. Catholic sex education being what it was and still is, I am amazed that more reflective and prayerful young girls and boys didn't end up as embittered young parents. Sex among teenagers in New Orleans when I was a kid in the 80's was a rite of passage held every weekend as we lined our cars up along Lakeshore Drive, and involved a series of ardent gropings and hesitant denials until the great wall of Papal resistance was finally scaled.

Thanks to Jimbo's news at that retreat, most of our girlfriends were put on the birth control pill by their parents in order to "regulate her period". Rhythm Method indeed, every one of my friend's parents knew their kids were going to have sex and they knew Catholic birth control was the biggest oxymoron in New Orleans after 'honest politician'.

Jess and I were roused from our thoughts as we made the final turn to Tim and Andy's and saw a life-sized mannequin that bore a striking resemblance to Ben Franklin, with the tell-tale bald on top long in the back hair and spectacles, dressed in late 18th century jacket and shirt on the top half and what could have been either Jayne Mansfield or Marilyn Monroe from the waist down in skin tight pink Capri pants and electric blue pumps. The mannequin's left hand held a ball of twine wrapped around a stick complete with a large skeleton key, while its right hand, daintily pointed to the right. Jess stared at the mannequin, her head followed it as it disappeared behind us. "What the hell was that?" she laughed as she turned back to ask me the question. I smiled back, "You know how people put signs or balloons up to show guests the way to the party?"

"Yeah…so? Oh is that what that was?"

"That's what that was, their version of giving everyone who needs them directions."

"Oh, man this is going to be one hell of a party."

"Yes it is."

The driveway to Tim and Andy's was lined with more of the same cross dressing hero's of the Revolution, John Adams was given a dimple and became Cindy Crawford, Thomas Jefferson was dressed in a seventies woman's pantsuit in order to fulfill his mission to become Bea Arthur as Maude, Paul Revere emerged as a Patriotic Lady Godiva, "riding" a crude horse with flowing blonde locks and holding an antique lantern in one hand while pointing the way to liberty with the other. Jess howled with laughter as we passed each one. I parked alongside the fifteen or so other cars that were filling up the massive side yard of the old house. Tim and Andy had done some work on the place since I had been here last. The place seemed brighter to me in the July sun, but it could have simply been the time of year. My last visit was over Christmas and the gray Gulf winters tend to give the houses along the coast a quiet malaise in winter that hibernates in reverse during the summer. Constructed largely of storm-felled cypress that was harvested from the local bogs and bayous, the house sits on thirty or so rounded stilts or pilings as they are known here, which are sunk deep into the soft ground and give the house a roughly fifteen foot lift over the nearby Pearl River, which has a tendency to crest whenever the rains get substantial. Meaning the Pearl is crested from April until October, so the height of the house, besides providing stature, also provides practicality and longevity. The ground was still a bit damp around the car as we stepped out, the result of last night's downpours. "Holy shit, this is some house," Jess stood, hands on hips and gave the place a good once over, "and this is their vacation place, not their real house?"

"Yep, during the week they live uptown, not far from me."

I answered Jess as I opened the trunk and pulled out 3 cases of Red Stripe Beer and a paper bag that contained two bottles of a 15 year old Haitian rum called Barbancourt, which I figure is patois for "drink this and then throw up". On the first sip the liquid slides down your throat soft and smooth as if it were on nothing more than on a Sunday stroll with happy sights of children and flowers and birds singing. When the rum descends to the lower regions of the bowels however, it expands as a captured fire does when an unsuspecting victim opens a door and exposes the starving flames to a fresh breath of oxygen. The rum's warmth rushes to the very ends of your body and consummates the union between spirit and flesh by forcing the first drops of sweat from your forehead, the back of your neck and your upper lip. It is only then that you begin to realize that you are in a battle for your soul and the only way to decide a winner is to keep on drinking. It is an entirely fantastic experience. I grabbed the beer, Jess took the bag containing the Barbancourt and we walked along the side of the house to speakers blaring Ethel Merman singing "You Can't Get a Man With a Gun" coming from the back.

Jess shyly dropped behind me as we turned the far corner of the house and got to the backyard where things appeared to be rapidly gaining momentum. The backyard, if you want to call it that, was nearly five acres of paths and openings carved into the pines that lead down to the bay. From the bay and by tricky navigation through a series of channels, you ultimately end up in the Gulf of Mexico. Laced among the trees were long lengths of red, white and blue piping along with great strings of lights that came in handy after the sun went down, the unstated truth of all of Tim and Andy's parties being that things would continue well into the next morning, regardless of anyone's need to get back to less important things like work, family or dialysis. Placed along the paths at regular intervals were large wooden boxes containing fireworks and cartons of kitchen matches that were available to anyone who wished to bring things in with a traditional bang. At the back of the house, where steps similar to the ones in the front led up to a deck that stretched the entire width of the house, a large American flag was draped over the railing of the deck and more red, white and blue piping wound around the house and down the handrail of the steps. More lights were accompanied by a last cross dressing historical mannequin, which bore an uncanny resemblance to George W. Bush, except of course for its retro punk fishnet stockings, leather skirt and knee high, black PVC jack boots. The President stood facing the flag on the railing, his right hand poised over his forehead saluting "Old Glory" while in his left hand he holds a large black dildo that bears a card saying "Weapon of 'Ass' Destruction." Jess walked over to "Dubya" and stood face to face, and gave him a good once over from top to bottom, she laughed loud and hard, "My father would shit a brick if he saw this!"

"So would mine." Tim said as he walked down the steps to where we stood. "Jessica I presume? I'm Tim Regan." Tim reached for her, kissed her cheek and turned to me, "Hanson, she's pretty, obviously well bred and smart **and** has a great laugh, what's she doing with you?" he laughed as he stepped to me, kissed me on the cheek and we hugged.

"My sense of humor of course, my mother always says I should make women laugh 'cause I'd never get one with my looks"

"Is that true?" Tim looked at her,

"Absolutely." Jess smiled that infectious smile that appeared to capture Tim as it had all the rest of us, he locked his arm into hers, "I'll introduce this lovely child around while you put that stuff away and please, please check on Andy and that wretched gas grill before he blows us all to hell…or Texas, which ever is worse." Jess and Tim disappeared around the corner as I ascended the steps to put the beer away and look for Andy.

Thanks to the hundred percent humidity, having to carry the beer, my middle aged spread, smoking or all of the above, by the time I got to the top of the stairs I had broken out into a full sweat which soaked my clothes through. I saw Andy and another man huddled in the far corner working to secure a propane tank to a brand new stainless grill that he and Tim must have bought for the event. Midway between him and us and square in the middle of the deck sat an elaborate Tiki Bar, complete with thatched roof and six foot Tiki statue that appeared to be frowning.

A tall, beautiful black woman was seated at the end of the Tiki bar that faced my direction and looked to be holding court over the six or seven people who had gathered around her. She spoke of the coming of the Mercury Retrograde, a period of the astrological calendar which is notorious for screwing up everything from machines to relationships. The woman chastised the crowd, warned them and informed them of the need to "lay low, not start anything new, not travel lest the trip be short and unprofitable…" her accent was thick and pure Jamaican which grew deeper and louder as she continued "…And beware of starting any new relationships during a Mercury retro-grade because they will most likely end in disaster…"

"Great." I thought to myself, but beat the thought back with the dour rationalization that Jess and I aren't even dating, less having a relationship.

My negativity was washed away when I saw Andy stand up next to the grill and rub his chin, having apparently just connected the propane tank to the grill.

"Either we are going to have one hell of a Bacchanal feast or the fucking thing is going to go up in one big ball of fire and take us, the house and that ass ugly Beau Rivage subdivision next door with it." He said to the man next to him

"That's optimistic" I called out to him. He laughed and stepped away from the grill.

"Go ahead and try to light it Tony." Tony, handsome, large muscled, hairy and dressed in a too tight white wife beater tank top, stood and stared at Andy before he cautiously reached for the propane tank and turned the gas on.

"Well, well Mr. Hanson, you've arrived just in time to for your parents to have to identify you by your dental records." When he heard that, Tony backed away from the grill and began to appear a bit nervous,

"You're sure you me want to light this? I mean we could cook inside," Tony stammered and lisped in a surprisingly high pitched voice meant for a much smaller man. Andy smiled mischievously back at him, "Oh, no we can't, Tim's got every burner on the stove going and the oven is full, so it is now or never, honey, fire this baby up, but just give me a second to get to the other side of the deck." Tony gave Andy a pathetically horrified look, Andy continued to bait him, "Oh, I'm just kidding dear, go right ahead, I'm almost positive it'll be fine." Tony smirked and finally understood that Andy was not going to let up and apparently decided that he'd rather face whatever the grill had to offer than listen to Andy go on and ignited the gas with a respectable "whooomp".

"Where can I put the beer?" I asked Andy as he cautiously examined the now glowing grill.

"We've got some big coolers just down this side of the deck and anything else left over can go in the fridge in the shed downstairs."

"Can you help me with them?"

"Sure, where's your new woman?"

"Jess is out meeting and greeting with Tim." I handed over some of the beer to Andy as he walked to the cooler and started loading them onto the ice. I reached for one already in the cooler as he worked.

"He's such an old Queen when it comes to meeting young women."

"Especially the ones I bring around."

Andy talked as he worked and didn't look up as he sorted the beer which took quite a while because cursed with a lifelong preference for absolute order, Andy wouldn't stop screwing with the beer until they were arranged just right. If he'd had the time, he would have inventoried and catalogued them as well.

"He just wants you to be happy...with someone he approves of, of course."

"And you? What do you want for me?"

"Honey, if I don't like her or I get a whiff of something that tells me she's going to fuck with you, then I'm on her quick and she's out the door." Andy, finally satisfied with the symmetry of the bottles and the nonchalant way in which the ice covered them, stood and wiped his hands on a towel that hung next to the coolers along with an assortment of penis shaped bottle openers.

"She's different Andy."

"Uh-oh...I think I need a drink."

"No, really, I mean...don't hold me to anything yet, Jesus, it's only been a half of a date."

"But I thought ya'll have known each other for a while."

"Well, yeah, as co-workers, but socially all we have is going out for one drink, and some making out by her car, but damn."

"I see..."

"Grab me another Red Stripe will you, you see what?"

"You're falling in love again." Andy carefully selected another beer for me, making sure to he kept everything just so in the cooler. I couldn't take his obsession any more, "Let me ask you something, don't you realize that as the day goes on people are just going to grab beers out of there however the fuck they want? And when they do, all of the other beers are going to get messed up."

"I do, don't be an ass. You know how I love clean lines and don't change the subject."

"I'm not changing the subject..." I took a big sip, the boiling heat, supported by the incredible lack of a breeze, especially this close to the Gulf has helped the second beer to taste better than the first, if that's at all possible. "...Well okay, I'm changing the subject, but what do you mean by 'again'?"

"How many times have you fallen in love since Liz left you for that doctor?

"I don't fall in love every time."

"Bullshit, you ready...?" Andy reaches for another beer for me, "You want a shot of Barbancourt?"

"NO! It's too early." Admittedly a half hearted protest.

"It's never too early dear."

"Fine." Andy handed me another beer and a penis to open it with and then reached into a cooler next to the one holding the beer and pulled out the Haitian bottle of hell that I've brought.

"Chilled just right," as he opened the bottle and reached for two shot glasses from a small table that was covered with them. To say the least, the rum was not disappointing. It settled in my stomach and then expanded like a dried sponge that had gotten its first taste of very warm and very thick water.

After the beers and the shot I began to feel a bit more relaxed, and realized that not having Jess around at that moment, not feeling the need to be "on" has opened the door for me to relax and be me. I looked out over the deck and found Tim and Jess walking among the guests out in the backyard. Tim appeared to revel in her company and acted as the proud host. I looked back over to the deck and saw that another group had gathered that included some of the production people who worked on a lot of my local shoots. I wandered over to them, but not before having reached for one more shot of the rum. As the second shot settled, I had begun to measure my steps, and approached the group as they were engaged in a heated discussion on divorce.

Nick, one of my lighting directors who, from the on set gossip I had been privy to on my last shoot, was going back to divorce court yet again, was already drunk, already bitter and being a shitty drunk, was already looking for an argument. Not surprisingly he spoke in the form of a yell, "You are never not married if you have kids." He looked over from the group and upon seeing me, he stood and walked over to me, his beer foamed and sloshed from the top of the long neck bottle as he placed a delicate hand on my shoulder, "Consider yourself lucky Johnny old boy, you got out without any. Julie and I have been divorced for five years now and Chris and Matt are still having a hard time and to make matters fuckin' worse she still gets on me for the same shit she did when we were fucking married fer God's sake. I told her the other day that she can't yell at me any more, and you know what she said?"

"What?" I replied, as I half listened and half watched as Tim and Jess walked up the steps, still arm in arm and joined the group.

"She said 'Fuck you!' and hung up the fucking phone, you believe that shit? Divorce is a fucking myth when you have kids. That's all I got to say."

"Yeah, but even if you don't have kids, you still never get away clean." It was Jess, "I mean, I have Amalee, of course, so Steven and I still talk... on occasion. But I have had long term relationships with people where we've broken up with no kids, no house, shit, not even a dog between us, and still I have lost a bit of myself, a part of me that I will never get back, a part of me that stayed in the relationship, a part that stays married."

I thought of the women, the relationships, the one night stands, and of course my one marriage. There is a lot of me left back there in the road somewhere. Finally, it was Tim that woke us from our collective malaise. 'Good fucking God I need a drink after that." We all laugh, both at the humor and at the opportunity to move on from thinking of the loss. I walked over to Jess and reached for her hand, she took mine, eased next to me and we walked away.

Nine

————◆·※·◆————

MY FATHER SITS on a cement and wood bench over near the electronic sliding doors that mark the main entrance of the hospital. Scattered around his scuffed penny loafers are the snuffed and charred remains of the half a dozen or so cigarettes that he has smoked since coming outside probably no more than an half hour or so ago. He rises and walks over to meet me in the parking lot and watches eagerly as I pull into a space and turn the car off. I open my door and almost step on him as I climb out, "You bring some beers?" he asks looking into the back seat.

"Yeah, I got a twelve pack, some ice and a Styrofoam cooler, it's all set up in the trunk."

"Thank, God, you know how hospitals give me the creeps."

"It's the smell." I say as I open the trunk and pull the cooler out.

"What're you doing?" my father had reached for the cooler at the same time as I did, but he apparently just wanted to take the top off and grab a beer.

"I'm taking the cooler out."

"Where the hell you gonna take it? It's not like we're tailgating at the Superdome"

"I guess you're right, you want to just leave it in the trunk?"

"Can we at least sit in your car with the AC on? It's hotter than twelve yards of hell out here, your AC works right?"

"Yeah Pop, but you got to roll the window down when you want to smoke."

My father has already opened one of the long necks with the bottle opener that he keeps on his key ring, and is hustling to the passenger side door when he turns and throws a look of disapproval back at me from above the car roof. "You gotta be shittin' me, what's the point in that?"

"Maybe if you're sweating you'll smoke less."

"Not likely." He throws the beer back and takes a big draught as he slides into the passenger seat spilling a little of the beer on his faded light blue "putter" pants. "Dammit." I hear him mutter as I open a beer for myself. Between what I drank last night, the three beers before going to my parents apartment, the drinks at Two-Two's and the beers sitting in the cooler now, I should be well on my way by the time I head up to see what condition my mother's condition is actually in.

"How's she doing?"

"Beats the hell out of me," My father takes another big gulp of his beer and reaches in his shirt pocket for his Viceroy cigarettes.

"What do you mean, 'beats the hell out of you'?"

"She's still in admitting."

"What!? Why is she still in admitting?"

"They can't seem to get in touch with Dr. Harris, and the guy taking over for him is in some tractor combine emergency or some other such horse shit, I don't know."

"Where's Mother right now?"

I catch myself as the question hangs in the air for the moment it takes my dad to drag on his cigarette, a long steady pull that wipes out half of the Viceroy in one breath, I realize that I'm not so much worried about mother as I am about how the hospital staff will perceive my father and I...again.

"She out cold and lying on a gurney in admitting, been that way since we left the house."

"Okay, so why are we outside drinking beer in my car? What if they have questions or something?" Again, other people's perception at play here, my mother could lay on that fucking gurney until the second coming for all I care, I take a sip and realize that I already need another. I open my door,

"Hey, while you're going...." My father calls after me and shakes his empty bottle back and forth in the universal sign of "I need another one." That first parking lot beer hits me so hard I have to hold onto the rear left quarter panel of my car in order to steady myself enough to open the trunk. Forget Brick's "click", 'cause he has nothing on me, I'm heading toward a full frontal, no holds barred, fuck up. I reach for two more long necks from the cooler and look back at the hospital as the exterior building and parking lot lights buzz once or twice, then light steady to bath the whole outside of the building in a cool blue stream and flooding the parking lot in their Xenon glow. Behind the hospital the sun breaks through the last of the clouds as it heads toward the west, bright orange banners shooting across the top of the facility's top floors, where somewhere inside, my mother still lays on her gurney, conscious or not. I wonder if she sees the sunset or would care if she saw another one. I toss one of the beers back into the cooler and walk back to my father's window. I hand him his beer, ice cold condensation drips down my wrist and onto his sleeve, "I'm gonna go in and see what's going on."

"Hold on Johnny," my father says, grabbing my wrist with one hand and taking the beer with the other, "You know how many times we've been here over the last year? Christ go even further back, to since before your brother died? It's not like I don't care you see, it's just that they know who she is, they know what her problems are, and they can handle her..."

"Yeah, but I just feel like someone ought to..."

"Then yeah, you're right, you go," my father interrupts, "because I'm sick of it Johnny, I'm sick of the smell, I'm sick of the people who wander the hall with their fucking IV's on those rolley stands that let them go wherever they want, I'm sick of a system that only cares about money, and I'm sick of the death. The whole place is consumed by death. It's in the creases of the walls and the grout of the tile, it's all porous, you know, the walls...the floors. They try and wash it away but they can't. This isn't any place to come get better, this is a place to come and die."

My father's grip has tightened to the point that I have to put my free hand on his to get him to let me go, I am taken back by his intensity, having figured my father to be somewhat passionless towards everything in his life. I just can't figure out whether when he says he's sick of it, is he sick of taking care of mother, scared of her dying, his dying or if he's just sick of everything.

"Fine. Then let me go in and see what's going on, you stay out here, put the radio on, maybe you can pick up the end of the Cub game you were watching."

My father lets go of my wrist and settles back into the seat. "Yeah, okay, that would be great, thanks." My dad opens the beer and turns the car on and then the radio as I back away from him and head into the hospital.

Outside of the main entrance, near my father's bench the rest of the smokers have gathered; visitors, staff and even some patients. All of them, particularly the patients, some of whom hold their cigarette in one hand and lean on those rolling IV's with the other, stare off into the distance, no one saying anything, all of them just standing, staring, absentmindedly inhaling and exhaling the caustic burn off of our nation's number one killer and doing it within six feet of a building where twenty or thirty feet above them someone is most assuredly dying from the very activity that they are partaking in. I stand and stare at them for a second, dumbfounded, being a smoker myself I certainly recognize my own addiction but even the most creative minds can't come up with irony like that.

The sliding doors whoosh open and I am immediately aware of the smell that I spoke of to my father. No matter how many times I come here, and dad was right we've been here a bunch, first with Harry and then Mother, the first time the smell hits, I want to run screaming. The smell is of antiseptic clean, accented with a hint of disease and dying, and every hospital, regardless of where it's located on the map, smells exactly the same. For in spite of all of their effort to sanitize themselves, hospitals are the number one place to get sick; a fluorescent, concrete and porcelain Petri dish of death and suffering. Now, thanks to an ill-tempered, impassive health care system, the hospital has become a place to do both without adequate care or even compassion for those whose prayers or profanities go largely unheard.

I see the sign that points to the admit area and walk down the hall in that direction. The hallway, at first narrow with long cork bulletin boards on both sides filled with notices about happy hospital activities like blood drives and memorial services opens up at the end where I enter an overly bright lobby area. Ten or twelve people sit slouching in two thirds of the fixed, hard plastic seats available, tossing and turning as I pass in an attempt to try and find an area on their asses that hasn't fallen asleep. Two black women in faded white uniforms sit behind the counter talking to each other while a third black woman works busily among a wall of files over their shoulders. A Pepsi Machine with a picture of Jessica Simpson on the front sits in the far corner of the room. She is appropriately dressed in hot pant shorts and a shirt tied at the waist slightly exposing her nicely shaped breasts. Next to Jessica's Pepsi machine, a Latino family sits huddled together, looking back and forth to each other, asking questions and answering in Spanish spoken with a hushed, nervous tone. Four years of "Modern Foreign Language" in high school and an acute deductive sense leads me to believe that they are apparently waiting to hear news about someone they've brought in. Two small children sitting on the floor at the grownup's feet fight over a toy that consists of looping and curving wires on which large wooden beads can be pushed through the loops and around the curves. The toy looks like a miniature version of an old roller coaster called the "Wild Maus" that my friends and I used to ride as kids at Ponchartrain Beach, the long demolished lakefront amusement park. Known simply as "The Beach", the park lasted for nearly sixty years at the apex of Elysian Fields Avenue where it met Lakeshore Drive on the shore of Lake Ponchartrain, until the land became too valuable on which to maintain such an archaic idea of fun, and the upper middle class neighborhoods surrounding it became consumed with the idea keeping "wild bands of nigger kids" as mother used to say, from passing through on their way to the park. The kids on the floor of 'Admit' are arguing now and a woman with a bloody bandage on her leg which shows through her torn jeans has emerged through a door and yells at them in Spanish, the kids immediately stop, the youngest one looking to and then toddling over to an old woman for comfort.

I walk up to the counter and stand waiting as the two women there continue working. And I stand. And I wait. Finally, the older of the two looks up at me, "May I help you?"

"If it's not too much trouble…" I begin, only now realizing that I am firmly ensconced in drunkenness, and deciding it best to flash my sarcastic wit, as I lean in pretending to need a closer look at the woman's I.D. badge "Mrs. Clark…could you possibly tell me what if anything has happened with Mrs. Hanson?"

"Are you related to Mrs. Hanson?"

"I am, in fact, her only living son. John Hanson, at your service" I extend my hand, to which Mrs. Clark shows a wonderful look of disdain.

"Well Mister John Hanson, what do you mean, 'What if anything has happened "with" her? Weren't you here when they took her up?" An able sparring partner in the war of words, Mrs. Clark is not about to cut me any slack of any kind. "After all some one should have been with her when the ambulance came in."

"That would have been my father."

"Where is he?"

"Out in the parking lot getting drunk in my car because he hates hospitals", *Take that woman.*

"Well so the fuck do I…" says Mrs. Clark as she reaches for my mother's file, the young girl next to her start to giggle. *Touché' Mrs. Clark, but we will meet again.* She opens my mother's file, lifts the 'pence nez' glasses on the chain around her neck to her eyes and scans the first page quickly, "…your mother is in 317, same room as always, she likes the view."

"How is she?"

"Why don't you go up and see for yourself?"

"I will." I start to walk away and a decidedly unpleasant thought occurs to me, I turn back to Mrs. Clark.

"You knew who I was all along, didn't you?"

"I sure did Mister Hanson."

"I'm an asshole aren't I?"

"Yes, you are."

"Thank you, Mrs. Clark."

"Anytime."

Humbled, and needing a drink I walk unsteadily back past the kids playing with the Wild Maus roller coaster toy, back through the hallway to the lobby and out the doors of the main entrance past the cigarette smokers, which of course makes me want to smoke and to get another beer from my trunk. Once back outside I realize that my short time in the air conditioning was a mere finger in the dike as the day's consumption of alcohol floods through me in the form of more sweat. The ambient heat, having conferred at length with the humidity has obviously decided that it is useless for the two of them to leave southeast Louisiana only to return in force again when the sun comes back up. Walking up to my car I can't see my father's head, which given his height, usually sticks out above the front passenger seat. It is only when I reach my trunk that I see that my father has reclined the seat as far back as it can go and is sound asleep. His beer, grasped tightly in his right hand, rests on his inflating and deflating stomach, a strong snore stifles the sound of a baseball game he has found on the am dial of the radio. Apparently unable to find the Cubs' game, it sounds as if the Astros are having a tough time against the Braves. I open the trunk and reach for a beer but stop short as I hear the announcer mention the name of a former high school teammate of mine who is pitching for the Braves. He was the number two pitcher for us my junior and senior years. He was number two, because I was number one. The only time in my life that I've ever been number one at anything. In New Orleans, fame in high school sports follows a person through out their life, constantly reminding them, at least in my case, of achievements realized long ago and of the more recent and the far more frequent failures of adulthood. To this day, twenty-something years since I last held a baseball in my left hand, I can walk into a sandwich place or bar or gas station and when I present a credit card to pay, the person taking the card will more often than not look at it, take a long pause from whatever it is they are doing, turn to me and say: "Didn't you use too?" or "Weren't you the guy who…?", Or "John Hanson? I thought you were dead", and despite the shooting pain in the middle of my forehead brought on by my own recollection of that time in my life, I am forced to smile and tell them that indeed that was me and as of now I am still not dead. Do I have something to show for the years that have past since to prove that I am not dead? Nope. A failed marriage and a failing liver, that's about it.

I close the trunk, open my beer and walk around to the driver's side of the car as my former teammate strikes out Craig Biggio on a fastball on the outside corner of the plate. The announcer remarks about my former teammate's velocity, his control, his determination to succeed all of which makes me want to puke because a lifetime ago he couldn't carry my shoes. But he made it and I didn't, and at the end of it all, when the last breath is working its way from the lungs upwards to the mouth to be spit out in anger, desperation or resignation, that's all that counts, he made it and I didn't. But I'm not angry.

My shirt shows the moisture seeping through front and back and under my arms, but this time they are accompanied not by nausea, but by a sense of loss and failure, failure as a man and failure as a person. Alcohol is a helluva mistress, she can either help you deal with ancient feelings and thoughts by filtering them into a golden glow, surrounding them the way the light softly surrounded the starlets of the early years of Hollywood, or she can run your memories over the grinding stone until their edge is as thin and sharp as a samurai's blade, eviscerating you and spilling your blood and guts all over the floor, and right now my mistress has me slipping and sliding all over my innards. Perhaps it seems that now may be a good time to go back inside the hospital and see my mother.

Ten

---•◦•◦•---

As IT HAS been said many times before, New Orleans is unlike any other city in the country, and not simply because of its wacky politics, "go cups" to take your drink from the bar to the car, Mardi Gras, beneath sea-levelness or the unique ability of its citizens to forget that there are generally 5 days in the average work week. New Orleans is unlike any other city in the country because it is the one place where people really don't give a damn about what a person does, either personally or professionally. For instance, Tim and Andy usually go to their camp over in Mississippi every Friday and stay there until early Monday morning when they pack up and drive the hour and a half or so back to the city where they trudge through the week just like all of the rest of us. Every Sunday they cook an enormous amount of food and every Sunday from one to twenty people show up to drink, smoke pot and hang out. On these Sundays the talk is intelligent, (even for Louisiana) varied and never ever allowed to drift into the realm of work or job, the worst of the "four" letter words. On the rare occasion a newcomer unfamiliar with the custom treads into the forbidden topic, they are grabbed by the largest among us and tossed headlong into the water as a reminder.

On the Fourth of July things are different. The crowd surges to the low hundreds (with over half of the attendees in drag), the conversation is bawdy and unintelligible (even for Louisiana) and the evening usually ends with the majority of the guests, regardless of what they talked about, swimming about in the paper bag brown waters of Pass Christian, either through their own choice or by being hauled to the end of the dock and ceremoniously dunked. This is after the performances of course.

By ten o'clock that night, the crowd had gathered on the lower back lawn and the lights strung in the trees had turned the dock into a multi-colored, cypress planked, star studded venue that even Judy Garland would have loved. Which she did by the way, as she was the headliner for the evening, though in the daytime Judy assumes the guise of a local sports broadcaster. Also by ten o'clock, Jess and I were well on our way to complete debauchery, aided by a continuous stream of Red Stripe Beer and punctuated by the all too frequent shot of Barbancourt. We had developed a slight rhythmic sway in our strides by the time we joined the other party goers and wandered the various circuitous routes down to the dockside show. We had lovely seats, mid-orchestra, center stage if you were comparing this to Broadway and near the bar which is definitely an active part of the theatre here. Tim saw us approach and as we took our seats on the finely trimmed, firm and scratchy St. Augustine grass that is so much a part of true southern living, he rushed over with a blanket, expertly tossed and spread it out for the three of us and collapsed in a heap next to Jess. The two of them chatted and giggled and I continued drinking until the lights strung about the faded cypress dock that formed the stage blinked on and off a couple of times and signaled that the curtain was about to figuratively rise.

If you have never been to a drag show before it is a marvelous event. I believe it is because there is an earnestness to drag performers that is lacking from the performances of the original artists; perhaps this is from the original performers having to repeat their own songs over and over, but I'm not sure. Each performance by an impersonator is an opportunity to actually become their heroine for just a few minutes, it seems to me that they instinctively reach for the brass ring each time. That earnestness was helped by the fact that the performers were able to lip sync, which took the stress of singing completely out of the equation. The suspension of disbelief was aided by the excellent costumes and wardrobe worn by the impersonators. It wasn't just Carson Fuller, a local production assistant who can't remember any detail whatsoever related to the commercial shoot you're doing and that he is supposed to be working on, but can, with little or no prodding give you the entire Alanis Morissette catalogue by song name, date recorded and registration number. That night, it was instead, Carson dressed and coiffed as the twenty-year old angst ridden, pissed off Alanis asking us if we think of her while we're fucking the girl that isn't her. It also wasn't State Representative Jimmy Gros, as Barbra in her best evening gown, slit up to the very top of his thigh, showing some very nice legs. And finally, to great expectation, came Ms. Garland, aka Mr. Jim Lagasse, owner, president and CEO of the Lagasse Automobile Empire, with over a half billion bucks of Detroit's finest sitting on all fourteen of his lots. Thankfully, he also has a half billion bucks of Japanese cars that he can actually sell. Jim Lagasse is the very epitome of old New Orleans society, rich, handsome and enormously gay. Jim chose the Judy Garland of the '60's for his portrayal. The later years of her life when the drugs and alcohol had beaten and aged her to the melancholy, tired, defeated person she had become. Broad dark rings highlighted his/her lower eyes; deep creases formed through his/her cheeks, which appeared gaunt and weathered, lines framed his/her eyes and mouth from years of smoking and gigging in the darkest of clubs. Jim's Garland wore a black A-line dress framed by a black cardigan and delicate black slip on shoes. His performance was exactly as I remember from a television special she taped not long before she died and the recording he used was, authentically, of the older Garland. Her voice full of the lost youth and innocence thanks to years of abuse at the hands of the studios. He was amazing, beautiful and ultimately as sad as she, and as he finished the last line, there wasn't a dry eye in the house. I looked to Jess and she was sobbing. Everyone stood and applauded wildly for Jim and for all of the performers as they took their curtain call. I reached out to Jess as we stood and she buried her head into my shoulder and then worked her way up my neck, and slowly, finally she reached her mouth to mine and we kissed for the first time since her car. The salt from her tears ringed her lips and she pressed her body heavily into me, eventually we parted, she wiped her eyes as she spoke, "I just want to crawl inside you, you are big and strong and when you hold me I know things are going to be alright."

"That's because they are." I told her.

It was then, at this moment of incredible tenderness, at this moment when she and I knew that there was definitely something very strong and very primitive between us that could define us as a couple and as individuals for the rest of our lives. It was at this moment that we were swept up by a group of drunken audience members and more drunken performers and whisked up the length of the dock and everyone all at once pushed/jumped/fell into the water. We surfaced together, and as she flung her arms around my neck she smiled, "This is by far the best time I have had in a long time...so are we sleeping here or at your place?"

"You mean together?" My eyes must have been bugging out like Marty Feldman's.

"Yes I mean together."

"Man, this is turning into a hell of a first date."

"But not really a first date, because the drinks after work were kind of a first date, but not really." she said as she let go of me and swam to the dock's ladder. "Is that what this is?" I said back to her as she turned, her gray eyes caught the light from the dock, her hair was flying everywhere even when wet and she flashed a very mischievous smile. "What?"

"Is this a real first date?"

"Yeah…"

"Best one I've ever had."

"Oh, it will be." She tossed, as she climbed out of the water.

"Here are fresh towels and clean robes, ya'll slip out of your clothes and I'll throw them into the dryer." Tim stood in the hallway of the house as Jess and I dripped on the deck.

"Ya'll slip out of your clothes where?" I asked, praying to God Tim wouldn't say exactly what he did say, "Right where you're standing honey, I don't want you drippin' all over my rugs."

"In front of each other…?"

"What are you getting so uptight about?" Jess laughed as I turned to see her already sliding her pants down. I looked, in fact, I'm sure I stared, and looking back at that moment as she casually undressed in front of me, it's a wonder that I didn't pass out. I did hyperventilate. Through my increasingly shorter breaths I couldn't help but to notice that she had an intricate tattoo at the base of her back, just above her perfect behind. It looked to be the face of a cat, or cats, I couldn't quite tell as she hopped away from me on one foot while she took her jeans off. But I noticed that the details of the tattoo trailed the width of her and wound across the tops of her hips, and all I could think was that good God almighty she had great hips.

"Johnny, you going to just stand there staring at her or are you going to take your clothes off?" Tim yelled loud enough for the entire Gulf Coast to hear.

I modestly turned and quickly took my shirt off, embarrassed of my body and not wanting her to see my paunch. Behind me Jess had already taken everything off, slipped the robe on and handed her wet clothes, including her underwear, to Tim.

"Come on honey, we'll let the Protestant get undressed by himself."

"You don't have to go!" I yelled defensively, "I can get dressed or undressed in front of anyone, just watch!" Tim walked over and put a hand on my shoulder.

"I'm taking this lovely and clearly uninhibited young lady upstairs for an Irish coffee, you come on up when you get done." He then turned to Jess who walked over and kissed me on the cheek, "I think your modesty is cute."

"I'm not modest, I can get naked with the best of 'em!" I blurted as she and Tim walked up the stairs. Still, being cautious, I walked over to the steps to make sure they had indeed started up before I hurriedly scrambled out of my pants.

Out of my wet clothes while having maintained my self-respect, I went upstairs into the open space of the house. From the sound of the voices that came from above it seemed that 20 or 30 other guests had remained past the annual end of the party dunking. The good thing about getting tossed in the water is that it appeared to sober everyone up, myself included. The stairs from the lower floor were made from wide, rough hewn cypress planks reclaimed from an ancient nearby landing destroyed when hurricane Camille tore through the Mississippi Gulf Coast in '69. At the top of the stairs was a great room off of the kitchen, a combination den and dining room that allowed expansive views of the water through house-wide windows and sliding doors that stretched from floor to ceiling. An eclectic collection of sofas and chairs were crowded with bodies, and everyone was drinking steaming cups of Irish coffee. I only knew one or two of the remaining revelers, so I pushed open the swinging door that led to the kitchen and saw Andy hunched over a Russian Samovar that he purchased for a run of "Uncle Vanya" at the St Mark's Theatre during the short period that he lived and worked in New York. He left after his love for Tim became the catalyst for a return to New Orleans, and as he puts it, his dream of accepting a Tony Award from Kristin Chenowith given up for a life of unequalled happiness. Tim and Jess stood in a far corner, huddled up conspiratorially and drinking coffee.

"'bout time Honey." She said as she walked over to me and kissed me, "I gotta pee, I'll be right back." She kissed me again and headed down the hall to the bathroom.

"Soooo?" Tim asked as he watched her walk down the hall.

"So what?" was the only reply I could think of, after all she had just called me 'Honey'...

"She is a great girl Johnny, none of the bullshit with the fake boobs, nose jobs and knock-off Chloe bag that you are known for, and she can actually manage a conversation."

"I absolutely agree...can I get one of those?" I asked as I pointed to Tim's drink.

"Certainly..." He grabbed a mug from the cabinet and told Andy, "Give him a good shot, believe me he's gonna need it."

I looked from Tim to Andy; they were obviously enjoying torturing me, "What the hell does that mean? What have ya'll been talking about?"

"Nothing...well, not nothing, but I want you to listen to me and don't get all defensive. This one, she's different from the others you've been with..." Andy said as Tim handed him the mug. Andy picked up the bottle of Jameson's first and held it over the mug for a count of at least twelve, and then filled the rest with coffee and chicory from the now leaking samovar and handed it back to Tim.

"Thank you Darlin'." Tim reached over and kissed Andy lightly on the forehead.

I looked down the hall toward the bathroom and of course started to get defensive;

"As I believe you've mentioned already, and of which you will be glad to know I am well aware of. But please elaborate and make it quick she'll be back here in a minute."

"Different in the sense that she just doesn't give a damn..." Andy continued, as he still fussed with the Samovar.

"Doesn't give a damn about what? Come on..." I continued to keep an eye on the hall, there was a line to get into the bathroom when she got there but I didn't see her waiting any more, so I guessed she was already in there and quickly tried to estimate how long she would be.

"About the things that your other girlfriends slash wife gave a damn about. "The Stuff" (he made the little open and closed quotes with his hands). You know, the house, the car, what clothes you wear, what clothes they wear, what clothes everyone else wears, what you say, what everyone else says, whether or not you wear that stupid earring we've been telling you you're too old for. This is one woman who appears to only care about two things right now, her daughter and you. So I'm telling you right here and right now to throw out all of that crap you think you know about women and just be real with this one."

"How the hell do I do that?"

"You've got to figure that out for yourself. Here she comes!"

"But...but..."

Jess came bouncing back from the bathroom, sipped her Irish coffee and dragged the belt of her robe behind her. I loved watching her; even with something as mundane as coming back to a party from the bathroom, she looked somewhat awkward, somewhat goofy and completely beautiful. I took a sip from my coffee, and only as it reached my lips did I realize that it was scalding hot. I tried not to let the intense pain show as I smiled at her.

"So." she stated with a confidence that sent a chill up my spine, "Are we staying here tonight or going back to the city?" I was dumbfounded; I plaintively looked at Tim.

"Here of course, in our best room", he smiled. I smiled in thanks back at him, I would've never had said anything or more probably have said the wrong thing, again influenced by a thousand years of Protestant belief that sex is only slightly less wrong than the two biggest sins, murder and converting to Catholicism.

"Will there be breakfast?" She smiled and looked my way as she said this. She is perpetually hungry and she knows that I know it.

"Absolutely, whatever you want." Andy called over his shoulder as coffee ran from the Samovar, dripped over the edge of the counter and onto the floor causing him to turn to Tim "Honey? What's Russian for 'Fuck this old son-of-a-bitch, I'm putting the coffee maker on'?"

Thank God for Tim's offer because at that point in the festivities I couldn't have driven the sixty or so miles back to New Orleans if someone would have spotted me fifty-nine of them. After having drank steadily for six or seven hours and then topped the night off with an Irish Coffee that would render most men useless, I had neared critical mass and the last thing I wanted to do was clip some cracker driving a Freightliner as he was coming out of the "76" Truck Stop in Slidell and spread Jess and I all over Interstate Ten.

"Well I'm ready to be tucked in, how about you?" she looked right at me as I stopped in mid-sip and developed a severe stutter at the same time. "Well…ummm…yeah…uh…"

"I'll show you where ya'll are for the night" Andy said.

He headed down the hall towards the stairs, turned left and went up to the second instead of down to the first floor. Jess followed and I trailed her as I was taught to as a kid. Follow the lady up and lead her down.

"Ya'll can stay in the main guest room, and I'll put any stragglers downstairs in the den." As we reached the top of the stairs the floor widened into two sections, on the left are the double doors to Tim and Andy's master bedroom and on the right, double cypress pocket doors that led to the guest bedroom. Andy threw the pocket doors open as Jess and I caught up.

"Cool doors…" She said as he slid the pocket doors all of the way into the wall, "…and what a great room!"

"It's French Polynesian." Andy said proudly." We picked up most of the pieces on a trip to Vietnam a few months ago."

The room opened impressively from the doors and covered most, if not all of that side of the house. In the middle was a tremendous hand-carved teak daybed, full of elephants, tigers and serpents. There were four columns that were shaped like great trees that rose from the corners and ended in a hand carved roof of massive leaves that formed a canopy over the whole bed. Mosquito netting hung from the corners. For some reason the musical the "Anna and the King" popped into my head, complete with a vision of Yul Brenner as the King and Deborah Kerr as Anna.

"Jesus, Andy, that's a hell of a bed." I managed as Jess ran to the side of the bed, and in order to get in had to climb as if she were a child boosting themselves into their parent's chair.

"I know, Tim and I saw it and just had to get it," He looked at Jess, "The serpents represent fertility of course." I shrank in embarrassment as Jess laughed and found the remote control for the TV and turned it on. My embarrassment turned to irritation because I hate televisions in bedrooms. And besides, if I was so un-appealing that she was going watch TV instead of wrestling around in a bed full of symbols of fertility, then I was heading home right then and there dropping her off and then throwing my set out with the rest of the trash.

"So, how are your parents?"

I looked at Andy quizzically as if to say 'What the fuck are you talking about, how do you turn off the television and why don't you leave?' He got it.

"You know what? Why don't you just fill me in on them in the morning? Well I'm pooped, I'd better shoo who's gonna shoo and give whoever's left a pillow and blanket." Andy turned and walked back to the doors, "Sleep well ya'll and thanks for coming today."

"Thanks for having us," Jess called back. Andy closed the doors and I walked over to the edge of the bed.

"This is the coolest room I ever seen and the biggest damn bed I've ever seen." Jess said as she sunk into the mattress and propped her head with the pillows.

"From the looks of it, I think it was meant to be outside." I half intentionally ran my hand along the length of one of the serpents

"Well…" as she pointed the remote at the television, "That's enough of that, you getting in this big son-of-a-bitch with me?"

"Yeah, let me go get the light first." I turned to walk the two or three miles back to the doors.

"I think that is what this one is for." Jess reached for another remote, pointed it at the lighted ceiling fan and the light went out. Moonlight peeked through a double French door that lead out to the balcony, but even in the semi-darkness I knew my way around. I had been in this room before at night, though never, ever with a woman and never with all of this teak. I walked over to the bed and clutched my robe closed as I got to the bedside; I climbed in and awkwardly slid under the covers. She reached for me.

"You still have your robe on." I turned to her and ran my hand along her side, "You don't…"

"No, I love being naked in bed." She smiled and wriggled under the covers.

"Really…" I don't think I've ever actually slept naked in bed in my life, preferring the socks on method for sex and sleep to prevent total nudity. My socks were down in Tim and Andy's laundry now though.

"Yeah, there's something about sliding into the cool sheets with nothing between them and me. Here let me help you take that off…" And before I knew it, we were naked, together, in bed…together. She was warm, almost hot to the touch. I used my fingers to lightly explore the length of her back from her waist up to her shoulder, I pressed slightly between her shoulder blades, she leaned into me and we kissed, long, slow, deep. The Irish coffees had given us just the right mix of both caffeine and alcohol. We were both alert to each other, but relaxed and unhurried. I kissed her neck and then her shoulders; I touched her breast and ran my fingers over her nipples, and found much to my surprise, that they were pierced. "Whoa!" I fought the urge to take my hand away from her.

"Yeah…" she says smiling,

"You didn't tell me that your nipples were pierced."

"It's not exactly a conversation starter, John. It's more like one of those things you find out after you get to know me."

"Yeah, I guess so. Hmmm."

"What?" Jess says as she leaned on her arm.

"I've never been with a woman who had anything pierced but her ears."

"So what do you think?"

"It's kind of cool, like you have little handles."

"Just watch how you handle the handles."

"You got it."

That was the last of the conversation. True to her tattoo she was feline in her motions, long lean pulls and pushes, her nails digging like claws on my chest and back, (the subsequent marks they left not healing for days afterward) and as she is when she walks, her movements in bed were in every direction at all times. Her noises were feminine and loud enough for Tim to remark about them days later. In a final push as she came, I felt her body tense and let go from her feet all the way up to her fingernails as she scraped them against the headboard of the bed, leaving long red trails of polish on the ancient carved wood. We lay with each other briefly after. I kissed her forehead as her body pressed against me and her head rested on my chest, we were both hot, sweaty and completely done, the sheets and blankets piled into the corner, neglected. "This was one hell of a first date."

"It sure was." She replied quietly, she turned away from me and I reached to hold her,

"Un-uh," she murmured, "…too hot." So I simply traced the lines of the tattoo and quickly with one soft girl snore escaping her, she slept. I laid awake for a minute or two, just long enough to trace her shape with my hand, just long enough to capture a picture in my mind that I knew I would keep forever, just long enough to know for sure that I loved her, and then, happier than I have ever been in my life, I slept.

Eleven

———◆•◆•◆———

WITH MY DAD sound asleep in the car and having taken a couple of Viceroys out of the pack in his shirt pocket, I stop outside with the smokers before going back in. I smoke them both in rapid succession. They burn my throat and the nicotine races through my blood stream. I feel it dispersing to the far reaches of my body, warming me the way the morphine did when I had kidney stones in college. I need the warmth to shield me against the hospital. Hospitals are always cold. I have never been able to figure out why that is. Maybe it has to do with disease, either preventing one from getting a disease or giving one to someone else. I have heard that the cold is meant to keep the patients in surgery from bleeding too much when they are on the table, but then why isn't it just the operating room that's cold? Maybe it has to do with the mental aspects of healing, as in the patients are so cold that they concentrate more on that than on the fact that for the most part they are getting very expensive, very mediocre care. What ever it is, the fact remains that it is fucking cold in hospitals.

My mother is in room 317 West, and as Mrs. Clark was nice enough to remind me, it's the same room she has occupied each of the 3? 4? times she has been in here since my brother died, though to be perfectly honest I wouldn't know her room from any other in this wretched place. I get off of the elevator, see the sign that lists the rooms by number and East or West, and turn right, walking past the Three West Nurse's Station on the way to my mother's room. The nurse's station is empty, leaving me to suppose they are all out giving medicines, checking patient's vitals and doing all of the other little things the hospital requires them to do so no one will get sued. But just in case someone does get sued, everyone can all say with confidence that the nurses did all of the little things that they needed to do.

I get to room 317 and hesitate briefly before going in because I can hear the television, and begin to worry that Mother might be awake, oddly enough, something I hadn't counted on. I ease the door open and peek slowly around the door as if I were Abbott and Costello or the Three Stooges and I was expecting to see either the Frankenstein monster or the Wolfman on the other side. Instead it is just my embittered elderly mother, all in all still pretty frightening. Mother lies stock still on her back in the bed nearest the door, the other bed, between her and the window sits stripped bare to the mattress and empty. Her eyes are closed, the covers pulled up tightly to her neck, her face looking more drawn and gaunt than usual, probably because of the harsh blue light of the bedside fluorescent lamp that shines obnoxiously bright, making me wonder how anyone can sleep with that thing on. From her wrist upwards extends an IV tube, Half filled with clear fluid, the tube coils around the head of the bed then terminates into the plastic bag that holds the saline solution or whatever else it is they're giving her. IV's always make me think of Randolph Mantooth and Kevin Tighe from the television show "Emergency", who, in numerous life and death situations as firefighters Gage and DeSoto respectively, called Memorial Hospital on the hotline and more often than not got Julie London, who played Dixie, the nurse, (who in spite of the fact that she was in her 50's when Emergency was on TV, was still so hot she had to be the model for every nurse character ever used in a porn film). Dixie in turn, received orders from a doctor, played by actor Robert Fuller, and then told Gage and DeSoto countless times to administer "…an IV with ringers lactate…" regardless of the ailment, regardless of the situation. As I stare back at my mother I desperately wish I could be off in Los Angeles, holed up in a suite at the Roosevelt Hotel with Julie London while Gage and DeSoto were here dealing with this now instead of me.

From midway down the bed another tube extends from under the sheets, I see my mother has a catheter that looks more than uncomfortable and comes complete with urine. Good for her, she deserves it. Mother isn't snoring, her trademark of deep sleep, but she does appear to be sleeping, so I walk quietly into the room and stop at the foot of the bed. I take a deep breath, and belch, bringing up a bit of the beer that churns away in my stomach for a second taste. It dawns on me that I have not eaten since the sandwich at my parent's apartment seven or eight hours ago and I'm hungry. I know that the cafeteria is closed but remember that there is a line of vending machines that stand along the wall leading to the cafeteria doors. I just turn to leave when I hear my mother's voice. "You going already?"

"Mother, I thought you were sleeping." I walk over to her bedside and kiss her cheek.

"Who the hell could sleep in this place? Besides they just came in to give me my medicines, they say I smashed my pelvis when I fell."

"Really." *What a fucking surprise you hard headed old...*

"Thanks for your deep concern, John." *Sarcasm as a word doesn't do you justice...*

"I am concerned Mother, but I haven't talk to the doctor yet..."

"And you think I'm lying."

"I didn't say that." I happen to notice self-consciously that I am backing towards the door. In a fight or flight world, with my mother I've learned it is always best to lean towards the flight end of the spectrum.

"Well I'm not lying, I knew something was wrong when they came for me, I could've told you."

Okay fine, I decide to give in, if she wants to go back and forth with me then, what the hell. I turn around, "Why did you try to get up by yourself?"

"I had to go to the bathroom, and the goddamn toilet was across the floor."

"Why didn't you wake me up?"

"Jesus, you didn't wake up when I fell, what makes you think I could've gotten you up on my own?"

"That's not the point Mother, the point is you're not supposed to get up by yourself, but you did anyway."

"So what you're saying is that it's my fault."

This is where it gets tricky with her, because what I really want to say is *'Yes, you spiteful old woman, it's your fault, it's your fault that you fell down, hell it's even your fault that your health sucks! Wake up and smell the fucking coffee, Jesus H. Christ, you've been wanting to die since Harry died five years ago so go ahead and die',* but instead I say, "No, mother, I'm not saying that, I'm just saying that you could've gotten me up to help you, and it's my fault for sleeping so soundly anyway." I walk over to her and kiss her on the cheek.

"Your father here?" she shifts uncomfortably in the bed.

"Yes, he's outside having a cigarette, you were sleeping when he came up." I lie, covering for the old man.

"Yeah, right, I don't sleep in the hospital, he's probably finishing whatever you were drinking. I can smell it you know"

I walk over to the door, "I'll tell him you're up."

"You do that," she starts twitching side to side, "...and on you're way out

have one of the nurses come in here, I don't think this catheter is in right…
it hurts like shit."

I close the door as she is still speaking and walk down the hall to the
nurses' station. An older gray-haired nurse is writing in one of the patient's
binders, "If you get a chance, could you look in on my mother?" The woman
stops her writing and looks up, I recognize her face, and she speaks without
showing any emotion at all, "Oh, she's awake then, what does she need?"

"She says her catheter is bothering her."

"They bother everyone, that's what catheters do."

I can't help but ask, "Have you looked after my mother before? Because,
she says she never sleeps when she's here." The nurse gets up and walks to the
door of the station, opens it and walks past me to go to my mother's room.

"Honey, I wish I didn't sleep the way she doesn't." Laughing I turn away
and go to the elevators to get my father so I can take him home to finally get
his own rest.

Sunday is the only day of the week where I actually have some sort of
routine. I get up early, go down to the local news stand and pick up the Sunday
New York Times, drive down to the Quarter before the tourists, still asleep
with heads full of Pat O'Brien's Hurricanes can get there and park illegally on
Decatur Street near the French Market. At Café du Monde I get two orders
of Beignets and two large café au laits to go and haul ass back home, where
I don't answer the phone or call anyone. Except for the few Sundays I spent
with Jess. During those six weeks we stayed in bed at the rental house until
lunch, then we would run out to a local grocery, grab po' boys and beer and
hustle back to the rental where we ate, drank and got back in bed.

When I open my eyes this Sunday all I know is that I just want to get
today over as fast as possible. I check myself for damage and am thrilled to
see that I have only the slightest hangover, which is a good thing. Hangovers
are truly the only downside of drinking, if you exclude things like DUI's and
cirrhosis. But all things being equal it's still not a bad price to pay for what you
get in return. If I am hung-over, my personal favorite cure is sex, preferably
with somebody, but, if necessary, porn or even a good Spanish novella on TV
will do. I think it has something to do with either getting your blood flowing,
so to speak, or simply focusing your mind on something else besides how bad
your fucking head hurts. Whatever it is, sex works pretty damn well. But
given the fact that I was very much alone and not willing to jerk-off in the
shower at my parents' apartment, I was glad for the fact that my hangover
was minimum at best.

I slept in the spare room at my parent's apartment and during the night
seemed to have jammed myself into the farthest corner of the bed where the
headboard meets the wall. Looking up, the first thing I see is my brother's

senior high school picture staring down at me. There are pictures of Harry all around the room; on the dresser, one from when he was just a kid, another when he was around twelve and playing Little League and another from his college years. On the nightstand next to the other side of the bed is a wedding photo, I'm not sure which wedding or bride, let's just say it's Harry and 'What's Her Name'. Then of course, there is the picture of him that sits on the television set. One that was taken closer to the time that he died, one that showed how tired he was; eyes sunken, cheeks gaunt, hair fully gray though he was only in his early 40's, the drugs and diabetes kicking the shit out of him and he, willingly kicking the shit out of himself by not caring. And then finally, if you search hard enough, you will see there is the one picture of me in the room, a fourth grade class photo, with bad hair and a worse expression that makes me look sort of like Bobby Brady after Greg has just beat his ass but good. It hangs dejectedly askew between the accordion doors of two small closets; the left closet has my parents' winter coats, the right one, still holds my brother's clothes.

I have never been able to understand my mother's adoration for Harry. All through school, elementary right up to and including his five years wandering the halls at LSU, mostly he was a loner, even to us. Once at LSU he rarely came home, even for holidays and Mother said nothing. When I decided to go to my college girlfriend's house for one Christmas in the three years that we were together, Mother complained to me that everyone else's family came first. On those rare occasions he did return for holidays, he was the mythical prodigal son. And yet, with all of that freedom he was never happy, except, maybe, for a brief time when he taught 9th grade history at St. Jerome's down in the Irish Channel. But like everything else in his life he just quit that too. For the first couple of years after St. Jerome's, he simply drifted through a series of useless, miserable jobs, all of them an attempt to prove or find something I suppose, but what I'll never know. I do know that he got more miserable with each and every crappy job, until the last one. The last job he loved, the last job made him so happy he wanted it to last for the rest of his life, which in effect, it did. You see, my brother's last job was selling pharmaceuticals, prescription drugs to you and me. He loved that job so much he took it home with him, and to the clubs and bars at night and to the golf course. His job went everywhere with him not because he was dedicated to his employer, but because was dedicated to his product. He was so dedicated that he got hooked on the very same shit he was selling. When the home office finally discovered that Harry was ingesting the samples that he should have been giving the doctors, so that the doctors could in turn hook somebody else, he was fired, no questions, no excuses. After that he gradually went downhill, looking for anything to get him off; cold medicine, shit stolen from the medicine cabinets of his few remaining friends, you name it. In the end, the combination of the drugs and the diabetes wore him out. Now, five years later, bleary eyed from drinking for most of the day before, I look at his pictures around the room and wonder that of all of the things that Harry wanted to be when he grew up, I'm betting an addict wasn't one of them. My parents never admitted to Harry's addiction though and when on one Saturday morning while Harry was still alive, I confronted them over his addiction, they turned a blind eye, preferring instead to continue to give him cash "to fix his car" or "pay his rent" or "buy him something decent to eat". I worked hard, took care of my bills and took care of my parents, but he's the one that got the love, not me, especially from her.

I hear my father moving around out in the kitchen so I get my khakis and shirt off of the floor, smell them, and lacking any other clothes, put them on in spite of their rankness and thankfully leave the room. Hoping against all hope that my father is having an eye opener, a Bloody Mary or morning Toddy, I am somewhat disappointed to see that he is just drinking coffee. But given that we have to go meet with mother's doctor, it is probably best that we do it sober, besides there's always this afternoon.

"Good Morning! How'd you sleep?" he gets up and hurries to the cabinet and grabs a mug from the lower shelf. The mug has an image of a cat drinking coffee and reading the paper drawn on one side of it and on the other side the words that say 'I'm having a pppuuurrrfect morning.'

"Fine, dad, just fine." It is only after I make my way into the little kitchen, where the window faces east and the sun comes raging in focused and hard like the beam from the eye of the great machines in Orwell's "War of the Worlds", forcing my eyes to dilate so fast I walk into the door of the laundry room and raise a welt just above my forehead, that I realize that perhaps my hangover was only playing possum, lying in wait for me to be eased into a sense of hope, only to spring on me and tear my eyes out from their sockets with one great sun-filled yank.

"Here, drink this, you'll feel better."

Ahhh, here's my headache; as the pain pushes on my skull from the inside out as if trying to escape the madness. "I could shoot my foot and feel better."

"I feel great myself, just chipper!" my dad smiles.

I have begun to notice in the last year or so, that for all of his demonstration to the contrary, my father seems to become a bit relieved whenever my mother goes to the hospital, but who could blame him? Twenty-four hour a day care for a person, even someone you love, has to begin to suck fairly quickly, I know I couldn't do it, especially for mother.

"So we need to go see Dr. Harris today, right?"

My dad bends over and opens the cabinet down next to the oven, grabbing a skillet and a cookie sheet,

"You want sausage and biscuits this morning?"

The thought of Jimmy Dean sausage making its way to a splash down in my stomach is almost enough to make me retch right there, "I don't think so dad, coffee will be just fine."

"You need something besides beer and coffee in your stomach, just have a biscuit or two."

"Okay fine, so we gonna see the doctor today?"

"Yeah, he's supposed be doing his rounds this afternoon around one, screws up my day though, the Cubbies game starts then."

As he talks my father has moved to the refrigerator where he takes out the cylinder of Pillsbury biscuits. He turns to the counter and as he finishes his sentence, peels the cover off, bangs the cylinder on the edge with a loud "whack!" splitting it open.

"What do you think he'll say?" I ask as he carefully places the individual pieces of dough in an orderly rectangle on the ancient cookie sheet, each piece an exact distance apart from the other.

"Hell I don't know, usually it's the same, the same condition, the same problems, she could live another two, three, ten years like this," he takes the margarine out of the 'fridge, " or she could go tomorrow, he doesn't know anything, I don't know anything…" He cuts the margarine into even squares and places one square on each biscuit, "…only she knows." He opens the oven and shoves the cookie sheet in, closing the door with an absent-minded slam.

"The paper is in the den by my chair if you want to read it."

He has effectively ended the conversation for now. He hates talking about her. Though that is not entirely true, the truth is he hates talking about anything. That's where I get the skill of non-communication. Actually it comes from both of them. In the forty years that I have known them, I have never seen them fight, and truth be told I never even really saw them have much of a conversation between the two of them. They always looked more at ease, more relaxed with other people. I remember as a kid having to go to bed on some Friday nights when my parents would entertain, usually work friends of my father's and one or two couples from the neighborhood.. I would spend hours sitting at the top of the steps listening to their conversations, their gradually raising voices punctuated by the sounds of ice in glass and cocktails being mixed and poured, beer tabs pulled, increasing laughter and eventually cards dealt. I sat there in my Jonny Quest pajamas looking down the empty steps at the closed front door thinking that all I wanted more in the world was to be down there with them, drinking and laughing. Harry, being older, would get to meet everyone, he would stand in the center of the room and answer endless questions about school and fictional girlfriends that existed only for him. Later he would come into my room and, seeing me awake would brag about getting to sip from our parents' drinks'.

My parents didn't entertain as much as they got older. They would hold an open house of sorts on New Year's Day, with the same people dropping by year after year for college football, cabbage, black eyed peas and samples from the mason jar of moonshine that my aunt would send from east Tennessee. The rest of the year they would go out to dinner, the same places and the same days of the week. Somewhere along the way, my parents just stopped. Maybe it was what they thought you were supposed to do, you live and have fun up until a certain age or a certain time and then you don't. I look over at my father as he sips his coffee and looks in on his biscuits as they brown under the expanding swath of margarine and for the first time in my life I begin to feel sad for him, and ultimately, almost incredibly, for Mother too. Not for the life that they have, but for the one they didn't have. For the first time, I see their life for what it is and what it has been for the last thirty years or so, passing in front of them like a silent train, noiselessly pulling hundreds of identical cars all full of the same kind of miserable cargo, with the origin so far behind that they have no memory of where they came from, and in the shrouded distance ahead of them, death as their only destination. "Biscuits are ready." My father calls, seeing that I am looking right at him.

"Okay Pop…" I answer, and I get up and go join him for breakfast.

Twelve

———⋄·•·⋄———

JESS WAS AN unbelievably sound sleeper, so much so that the next day, Sunday, the Fifth of July, I was able to get up, get out of bed, go to Andy and Tim's laundry room, get our clothes, (which were nicely folded on the dryer), go back to the room, get dressed, leave her clothes at the foot of the bed, kick the bed, muffle a scream, grab my right Pinky toe, whimper a lot and still not wake her up. As I walked out of the room again I looked back at her, half covered, she laid on her stomach, her left leg stuck out from under the sheets, her foot hung over the edge of the bed, and as I closed the door, a very nice snore came from somewhere under her mass of wild red hair. I hobbled out to the kitchen, and found Andy slumped over the counter, a shiny copper coffee pot had just begun to percolate on the stove, the milk warmed in a pan next to it.

"You okay?"

"No." Andy's mouth barely moved, a small puddle of drool had formed where the corner of his mouth met the counter top.

"You want to go lay down on the couch? I'll watch the coffee…"

"I'm afraid that if I stand up, I'll just collapse in a heap on the floor, besides the counter is very cool on my face." I walked over to him and eased his head off of the counter and looked him in the eyes.

"You're still drunk."

"Thank you for that update darling, I wouldn't have guessed on my own."

"Shouldn't you go to bed?" I ask as I walk around Andy's talking corpse.

"I can't, Timothy's parents are coming out for a barbecue later today and I have a ton of things to make, his dad absolutely adores my chocolate pecan pie you know." Andy leaned up with that last line and waved his mug around in the air, his middle finger secured it through the handle. "Here, give me that and I'll actually put some coffee in it." Andy handed me the mug,

"Sooooo, how was *your* evening, mister?"

"What evening?"

Andy laid his head back down onto the counter, "Oh, come on, don't be coy, I do the laundry around here so I'll know about it sooner or later, give me some details…"

"That's gross and I'm not going to give you any details, you want sugar?"

"Did you put the sugar in first?"

"No, I put the coffee and milk in first."

"Pour that out and put the sugar in first please, I like the way the coffee dissolves the sugar when it gets poured in. So wasn't it any good? The sex that is."

"Jesus, you're fussy…I figured you weren't talking about the coffee and yes, it was great, but I'm **not** giving you any details."

"Fine, I'll get them from Timothy, you'll tell him, you like him more."

"Here…" I placed the coffee into Andy's out stretched hand, "…be careful it's hot, and I love you both equally."

"But you'll tell him."

"I won't tell him, he just has a way of getting information out me."

"Don't worry about it, he gets things out of me too darlin'"

"That's nice…Cool it, here she comes…" I whispered to Andy.

Jess walked down the hall to the kitchen. She had eschewed her own clothes for an oversized man's blue Dickie's work shirt that bore a red trimmed white oval over the left chest pocket, the name "Hap" was stitched in red in the center. Her hair looked as if it were electrically charged. Andy turned, "Well good morning sunshine, and don't you look lovely…Medusa thy name is 'Hap'," then reached over to her and kissed her on the cheek.

She stifled a small yawn. "You're still drunk." Andy stepped back as if he were accused of pinching her ass,

"You say that as if it were a bad thing," he sounded in mock surprise, "Can I get you and your hair some coffee?"

"Very funny smart-ass, and yes you can." Jess walked over to me and kissed me very lightly on the lips.

"I haven't brushed my teeth yet." Jess said.

"So what" I mutter as our lips meet.

"Your breath is probably no worse than it was last night." Andy said to Jess as he returned with her coffee.

Jess smiled at him "You're such an old queen." Which made Andy howl and wrap her in a big hug.

"You are a dear, Johnny if you don't sweep her off her feet then I might let her sweep me off of mine. And now, I need to nap. You two, the house is yours." Andy eased into a half-curtsy, "Adieu, mes amis" then turned and walked gracefully right into the wall.

"Nice exit," I said.

"Bite me Hanson," Andy tossed back as he walked down the hall. Jess and I watched him as he managed by reaching out with both arms, like a slightly effeminate member of the Flying Wallendas walking the tight wire high above a crowd.

"You have a couple of really great friends in those two." Jess kept her eyes on Andy.

"I know, when my wife left they were the sympathetic aunts I never had. They were much nicer about it than my mom."

"Why? What did she do?"

"She told me that my marriage lasted a hell of a lot longer than she thought it would."

"She did not."

"She did."

"Really?"

"Well, sort of, she said, that it lasted longer than most."

"That's a little nicer."

"A little, you want to get out of here?"

"Yeah, I'm starving." I took her hand and headed her back in the direction of our room.

"You're always hungry...you eat as if you're on a food bender, but you still weigh twelve pounds."

"I do not, where are we going?"

"Back to the room to get our stuff, and then we'll go get breakfast, there's a bunch of mom and pop places over on the old state road that goes to Biloxi."

She stood on tiptoes and kissed me on the neck, "We don't have to go right away you know."

We kissed until we got back to our room, convened inside quietly and not too quietly for some time until eventually emerging around noon to loud cheers from Tim's family and when pressed into sitting for midday dinner, decided to extend our stay another day.

Thirteen

——◆·❖·◆——

I HAVE DECIDED to leave my car at my parent's apartment and ride with my father to see mother's doctor. I am not in any hurry to go back into New Orleans today. If I hurry home today, then before you know it today will become tomorrow and Jessica will be at work tomorrow. Hence, the longer I can put off dealing with that the better I'll feel and trust me when I say that nothing stretches the day like a Sunday in Brentwood, Louisiana. Even though it is summer, and damn hot in every corner of every town in the southern part of the country from San Antonio to Miami, it seems that the heat holds a little something in reserve for Bentwood.

As my father weaves his Pontiac Sunbird through the narrow streets (made narrower by the presence of the obligatory extra large, extended cab, pick-up trucks with the occasional rebel flag or Gospel verse, notably John 3:16, stuck to the rear window), the sun seems to get a running start, building up speed as it approaches the bleached white cement streets, only to move faster still as it bounds off of the street and blows through the middle of my head like a red hot steam engine. I cannot keep my eyes open for fear of having them melt from their sockets, which, when I think about it, is not so bad after all as it keeps me from having to look at one dingy subdivision after another. My father finishes his cigarette, tosses it out of the window, hacks out a cough, spits the phlegm onto the street, much to the disgust of a couple of kids on bikes, and turns to me, "In case you're wondering, I'm taking the back way to the hospital, that way I miss that light on highway 11".

"However you want to go Pop, you know this place way better than I do" I say, fighting off nausea caused by his hawking of the mega lugie.

"Why are your eyes closed?"

"'Cause the sun is so goddamn bright I can't keep'em open."

"Where are your sunglasses?"

"I don't know, why are we going to meet Dr. Harris at the hospital?"

"Because it's Sunday and he doesn't keep office hours on Sunday, but his service said he is doing his rounds at the hospital. Most Sundays he's off and it's one of the other doctors in his practice that covers the hospital. The last time your mom was in it was some Indian woman."

"India Indian, or American Indian?"

"India Indian."

Immediately a Bollywood image of an attractive Indian woman shedding her sari for an operating gown while singing some undecipherable song about losing her love while gaining her independence only to find it all so unrewarding and lonely goes through my mind.

"Your mom didn't like her one bit".

"I'm shocked" not caring to hide my sarcasm.

"Your mother isn't a racist John."

"No Pop she's not…she's a bigot, there is a subtle difference."

"Your mother likes people of all colors."

"You're absolutely right…as long as it's hers."

"Stop it now!"

"Yes sir" I snap back like a dazed marine recruit. The exchange reminds me at how my father's voice, when raised, can instantly transport me back to my childhood, to that time when I still respected and feared him and before I grew to know his behaviors and his own fears that were the source for them. After that revelation, my respect, almost overnight turned to anger at his weakness; his weakness with Mother, his weakness in giving in to Harry, his weakness with alcohol and ultimately his weakness with life in general. I also became angry because in spite of how much I may have denied being anything like him, I saw those same weaknesses in myself. The rest of the ride to the hospital was in complete and total silence, which just so happens to be the natural state of co-existence for he and I.

Dr. Donald J. Harris stood in the hallway of floor Three West speaking with, from what I could over hear of their conversation, a person that appears to be the relative of a woman in a room two, or three doors down from my mother. It has been seven or eight months since I've seen him last and he is taller than I remember and seems at this moment to be standing on his toes, perhaps to increase his authoritative presence. He looks like the stereotypical Florida Plastic Surgeon. Smooth talkers with gray hair, a perpetual tan and the kind of smile that only comes from long hours of hitting on women in weird little bars that have cute tropical names like "Sandi Beach's" and serve ten dollar martini's. All with the intention of getting those women to their slightly pre-owned Porsches, so they can spend most of the evening wrestling with them on the overstuffed leather couches of their two mortgage, not quite as beachside as they lied to the women, condos. I can only hear every third word of what Dr. Harris is saying but it sounds as if he is telling the woman's husband/son/uncle that she is going to need some sort of surgery, he is smiling the Porsche smile as he says it. Harris turns to see my father and I, gives us the very same smile with a pope's wave for effect and I take it to mean that he will get to us whenever he damn well pleases.

Father and I walk into my mother's room to find her sitting up, shaking and IV laden hand at the television and yelling at Terry Bradshaw, Hall of Fame former Pittsburgh Steelers quarterback and three-time Super Bowl Champion turned sports caster.

"What the hell do you know you goddamn redneck!"

"Good morning Mother!" my father chirps to her. She doesn't answer as her eyes never leave the television screen, the audio screeching from the wired mini speaker resting on her pillow as if she were not in the hospital but sitting in her bed in the drive up lane at any one of the million or so fast food restaurants in Bentwood.

She turns to me, "I want to know why, if an ignorant bumpkin like that guy is able to get on television, you can't manage to keep a wife or get out of New Orleans." I kiss her on her cheek, "I don't want to get out of New Orleans mother".

"Yeah, well you were never the bright one, you here to watch the game with your poor ol' mother?"

"No ma'am, we're here to see Dr. Harris," I answer knowing full well my father probably hasn't told her and after her nasty greeting, desperately wanting to stir the pot. Mother likes to deal with her doctors on one to one basis, that way she hears what they have to tell her and then has time to think up whatever lie she wants to tell my father and I later.

"What the hell for? I can talk to the goddamn doctors!"

"I know you can Mother…" my father stammers, shoots me a look and immediately begins performing the ritual of denial known in these parts as 'crawfishing', "…and we did come by to watch the game," he continues, trying to regain his footing, "but since we saw Dr. Harris out in the hallway, I figured we might have a word with him."

"Bullshit, you don't think I'll tell you what he says?"

"Will you?" I ask, pouring gas on the fire.

"Stay out of this," my father lashes out at me. "Look mother, I don't think you'd lie, but I'm not sure Dr Harris would tell **you** all of the details, so I thought it would be best for John and I to talk to him while you watch the game." My father plays her well, knowing her love for football and her addiction for the Saints.

"Aw screw 'em!" she screams, her attention back on the television. "Why do I waste my time on a team whose claim to fame in forty years is one field goal kicked by a half-footed, no-handed kicker who was put in there by a coach who couldn't think of anything better to do?"

As Mother speaks I am so desperate to get away from the here and now that I do, and drift off to November of 1970 and that game between the Saints and the Detroit Lions. The greatest event in New Orleans sports history (arguably, of course, because there was also the night the late "Pistol" Pete Maravich scored 68 points for the former New Orleans, and now Utah Jazz against the New York Knicks) is recalled by Saints fans the same way some people recite Clement Moore's "Night Before Christmas" on December 24th and occurred in the final seconds of a meaningless game when Tom Dempsey trotted onto the grass of old Tulane Stadium, looking more like a teamster than a athlete. The Lions, as the legend goes, almost laughed themselves off of the field, when it was revealed that the Saints were going to let this poor fat man try a field goal from the unfathomable distance of sixty-three yards. Joe Scarpatti was the holder, Jackie Burkett was the center, their names emblazoned in my mind as much as Dempsey's. The ball, incredibly, was placed on the Saints own thirty-seven yard line. I remember listening to the game with Mother and my friend from next door Danny Ford, when just before the kick, the radio went dead (rumors were that bees had swarmed the station's transmitter, this was the Saints after all and nothing is out of the ordinary). Danny ran home and came sprinting in the back door with a transistor radio he'd taken from his dad's boat blaring as the announcers were screaming hysterically that Dempsey had indeed made the prodigious attempt. Mother, Danny and I embraced and screamed as well. My father, who attended the game, had given up hope just minutes before and missed the whole event, preferring to get a jump on the crowd and smoke a cigarette on the exit ramp on his way to the car.

"Well now how are we today?" It's Doctor Harris' voice that propels me back to Mother's reality.

"You're just fine and I'm stuck in this shit hole." she blurts.

"Good to see you're as feisty as ever Jean Anne, let me have a look at your x-rays" Harris reaches into the envelope at the foot of the bed that holds mother's x-rays, I try peaking to see if they cover enough of her chest to show that she truly has no heart.

"Oh good, you broke your pelvis" One of the more pleasurable qualities of Doctor Harris is his willingness to give back to mother the shit she gives out.

"How did this happen? He says peering over the x-ray at her.

"She tried to get up on her own." My father jumps into the fray with a shot across her bow to get Mother to settle down.

"Hmmm Okay…how come you did that Jean?" Harris is a born and raised New Orleanian and his lengthy heritage shows itself in accent and word order.

"I missed you." Mother snarls back at him.

"Well it seems that we will be seeing a bit of each other for a while. How's your feet doin'?" One of the major problems with diabetics is that their circulation begins decreasing rapidly to their extremities, and mother was no exception. Her feet were at their best a dried and bloody mess and at their worst dangerously close to gangrene and amputation. Right now some sort of air cast covers her right foot and extends up to her knee and I'm guessing things aren't too pleasant under it. Harris gently removes the cast to look at the foot, a bandage wraps around the middle securing a large gauze pad on the underside. Harris takes his snub nosed scissors from his right coat pocket and cuts the bandage across the top of her foot and eases the wrapping and the gauze from the underside. With the foot exposed I can see an area of blue-black skin, or what was skin, covering the bottom. In the middle of the dark area the foot appears to be splitting apart at the seams exposing deep tissue that also appears to be a deep blue-black color. My stomach churns to see so much rotting flesh and I turn away appearing to watch the game. Dr. Harris frowns as he looks at her foot and then turns to me, "Can you reach me that gauze and wrap from your momma's cart over there?"

"Oh, yes sir." I chuckle at the sound of someone calling mother 'momma' a local term of endearment. I can't imagine this woman as anybody's 'momma'. I hesitate slightly for some reason before retrieving the materials needed to replace mother's bandage and handing them to Harris.

"Okay Jean, I'm going to re-wrap this and then we can talk." The doctor's hands move swiftly with the bandage. He passes the time chatting "So, this is the first real game of the season right, they're playing Atlanta?" Harris is addressing me, though I'm not listening and clearly have forgotten myself that I am even looking at the television as my mind has wandered to the singular thought of getting the hell out of the hospital and getting a drink.

"Yeah…" I say finally. I feel like I am operating on what seems to be a six-second delay, like the "live" television that we're watching, but not seeing. "I haven't kept up with them though, I've sort of lost interest" I mumble back to the doctor, and isn't that the truth? What have I thought about in the two months that have passed since Jess? Drinking? Yes. Internet porn? Yes. Getting the hell out of my life in an attempt to run away from the muck of anger and depression that I feel for everyone and everything in it? Absolutely.

"That's too tight!" my mother's complaint echoes out of the open door and into the hall.

"I'm right here Jean, you don't have to shout." the doctor says with patience. I just want to run out of here. Harris turns to me, "I don't blame you, ever since they got rid of that kid from McNeese State and kept that black son of a bitch at quarterback, they haven't done shit."

"They did it 'cause most of their fans are black." My dad chimes in, I see where the conversation is headed. I have to get out of the room before they start lighting crosses.

"You need anything Mother?" I say backing towards the door.

"A vodka and tonic, a Lone Eagle sandwich from College Inn and a cigarette."

"How about a diet Coke instead?" I answer turning for the door.

"Don't go far," my father tells me, I turn to see his face, his eyes plead to me as if to say 'don't abandon me here, don't make me face another useless conversation about what my or may not be, and will only damn me to taking care of her.'

"I'm just running to vending by the cafeteria on two, I'll be right back."

"Bring me a diet coke!"

"Yes Mother"

I step into the hallway still hearing my mother's voice behind me, barking at the television as the game plays. Walking down the hallway to the stairs takes me past the other rooms and though I try not to, I find myself looking into the ones that have their doors open, mostly to see if other families have to deal with the same madness that we do. The rooms are mostly quiet, except for the televisions of course, and though I look to see the patients, it is the visitors that I notice. Most of them sit next to the beds in those terribly uncomfortable chairs that they have scooted close. Those few who are visiting the ones that are actually getting better laugh and talk loudly as if to boast of their good fortune. Those who visit the ones whose health is declining turn their faces out into the hallway, their skin bloodless and their eyes hollow and dark from not sleeping. They look to the passersby as if begging for a reprieve from their deathwatch through either a miracle cure or death itself. All of the rooms seem as if frozen in a diorama of the nameless for whom time passes slowly. The second hands of the wall clocks in each room advancing with a great loud 'TICK', reminding everyone of that which is, as Faulkner called it, time, man's ultimate mausoleum.

The door to the stairs is blocked briefly but opens as a doctor and nurse walk out onto the floor chatting of a vacation to the Caribbean. I emerge from the stairs onto the second floor near the cafeteria and even here the smell from the hospital overcomes even the strongest aromas that rise from the food as the lunch service begins. Tables are slowly filling with staff, visitors and patients in wheelchairs and their intravenous shadows. I get my mother's diet Coke and make it back up to her floor in time to catch my father and Doctor Harris walking down the hall. I have been here often enough to recognize the room they turn into as the small chapel the staff uses to give families bad news. I stop at the door to my mother's room long enough to hear her characteristic snoring, indicative that she has fallen into a deep sleep, the Saints game still blaring from the bedside speaker. I twist open the diet Coke, take a sip and walk to where my father and the doctor are speaking.

"Her kidneys have been getting worse for quite some time Sean, this really isn't anything new, just a progression of her condition." The doctor stands, his back against the far wall, his arms folded. My father sits in the lone chair, elbows on knees, his hands spread across his face.

"What did I miss?" I ask, my father's hands drop from his face and I can see that he is actually crying, I stare for a moment, mystified. Doctor Harris, seeing me, fills me in, "I was just telling your father John that I am not holding out a whole lot of hope for your mother to make the end of the year."

"What?"

"Her kidneys are failing rapidly, she's been in congestive heart failure since her kidneys started giving her trouble two years ago making her circulation extremely poor, her feet are horrendous, it's a fucking miracle and a testament to your father that she doesn't have gangrene. And in spite of how she behaves occasionally I really believe that she is slipping into dementia as another result of her circulation problems. As you know she does have a broken pelvis, but considering how little she moved prior to her fall I don't think it will impact her all that much. I can't justify keeping her here more than a couple of days and she is beyond what you can do for her at home Sean."

"So what do we do?" I ask, noting my father's look to me as I used the pronoun "we".

Perhaps as a awareness to my own apathy, Harris turns to my father, "Sean, she needs enough care to keep her from suffering too much, over the next few months. Do you and Jean have any sort of long term health insurance, something that will allow you to put her in a nursing home?"

"No, we had to cut some things out to give money to Harry."

"Jesus Christ…" I walk out into the hall and back in, wanting to hit something.

"Not now Johnny."

"How many times can one person ruin our fucking lives Pop? Every time you guys need something, every goddamn time its like he reaches up from the grave and takes from you again."

Dr. Harris has worked his way passed me to the door. "Sean, ya'll have a bit to talk about, I'll leave word at the nurses' station to have the social worker give you a call."

My father jumps up and grabs Harris' hand. "Thanks Doc, we'll get it straight."

I barely wait for Harris to leave the room, "What the hell are we gonna do Dad?"

"I don't know Johnny, I just don't know, but we can't fight about this and we can't fight about Harry. We are where we are, and we just have to deal with it."

"But we shouldn't have to..."

"That's enough."

End of discussion, "Yes sir..."

"I'm going back to your mother's room, come tell her bye and get on back to New Orleans, I'll call you after I talk to the social worker."

"Okay, dad." I look at him, it is these moments; the ones where I feel like we ought to hug or tell each other 'I love you,' or in some way express some sort of emotion to one another, that I realize how little true feeling passes between us. I walk with him back to mother's room, where she still snores placidly. My father walks to the corner of the room, past a nurse's aide who prepares the bed near the window for a new arrival and pushes mother's wheelchair from the corner to her bedside, picks up the remote control for the television and sits down. "I'm gonna go dad."

"You want me to drive you to your car?"

"No, I'll just call a cab from the nurses' station." I start to walk out of the door.

"You going to kiss your mother good-bye?"

"Yes sir." I look over at my mother, she has stopped snoring for the most part, her thin gray hair has matted against her forehead, she is covered in sweat despite what I consider to be the numbing cold of the hospital, her mouth lies open, her top teeth removed. As I lean over her I am reminded of images of Egyptian mummies from a National Geographic article I had pored over as a kid, describing in detail the process for preserving the dead. The part that comes to mind looking down on Mother now is where they described how the priests or whoever performed the mummification would reach up through the nose of the dearly departed with a long hook and just sort of tear and drag the brain out through the nostrils. I shudder as I kiss her forehead.

I roll up to my parent's hovel in the faded velour backseat of a 1990 Seville a from Bentwood Taxi held together by prayer and Bondo at one o'clock and immediately decide that I need at least a drink or five with lunch as a cleansing ritual to wash away the feeling of death that clung to me at the hospital before I can drive back across the lake. Lacking any formal knowledge of the town because I have, for the last ten years or so, managed just to drive straight to my parents' or to the grocery, I head back to the only place I know.

The sign out front of Tu-tu's announces a deal on their "famous" Sunday champagne brunch, which includes a free bottle of champagne with your meal. The restaurant's lot was full so I park in the mostly empty parking lot of the Lutheran church next door and shutter to think what form the champagne at a place like this would take as I shut the car off and walk in. As my eyes adjust from the blinding sun into the cool darkness of Tu-tu's I find that most of the customers are not eating the 'famous' brunch, but surrounding the bar and yelling at the television in an effort to impart a sense of urgency on the Saints who are losing once again to the hated Falcons. I see an opening at the end of the bar where the wait staff picks up drinks for their tables and move myself in. Harley is back behind the bar, but today a thin girl dressed in a Saints tank top and jeans accompanies him. Her exposed arms reveal tattoos that run from shoulder to wrist and appear to me to be either a representation of the Last Days with Jesus Christ peering down at the burning planet from her left shoulder, or the live audience at a taping of American Idol . Harley gets to me first, "Beer and a Jameson?" he shouts placing a bar napkin in front of me.

"Why the hell not?" is the only thing I can think to say. Deftly he places a pint of beer and a shot of the Irish whiskey on the bar in front of me. I hesitate briefly, holding the shot up in front of me and looking at it with the feeling of both dread and anticipation. I drink it quickly and allow the whiskey to expand and warm me before taking a large sip of the beer to cool me off. Again I assure myself that I am in no hurry to get home, convince myself that though I know not a single soul in the place I am indeed, thanks to our current commonalities; that being a willingness to drink on 'The Lord's Day', and scream at the television, I am surrounded by friends. Emboldened by that, I order another shot and commence to build the wall of artificial self confidence that I will need to make it through the rest of the whatever.

Fourteen

———◆◄►◄►◆———

WHEN JESS AND I finally returned to the office after July 4th, it was everything I could do to hold inside what was going on between us. I thought for sure that someone would notice the difference in me, the way I seemed to find things to meet with her about, either in her office or mine or just the way I was always happy. Could it be just coincidence that we managed to go outside for a cigarette at the same time, or walk down St. Charles Avenue to Clean Charlie's, the neighborhood bar slash diner slash laundromat for lunch? One of my favorite things to do with her was to sneak out in the middle of the day for a shot or two of Jameson's at a local place, run back to the office, and then power out the last couple of hours under a nice buzz. While I was the happiest that I had been in a long time, I had no clue what to call the new "us" and I wanted a label, I really wanted to brand whatever we had, after all this is what I do for a living, brand things. Plus I wanted something concrete to tell my friends, something to brag about. I finally asked her one-day at lunch about two weeks after the party.

"Don't ask," Jess answered between bites of white beans and rice, "because I don't know what to tell you."

"Well…" I pushed hesitantly, "…are we dating? We did go to the movies, so it's not like it's all just drinking and sex." Though to be honest, that pretty much defined the first two weeks, it seemed as if we had sex at every opportunity, which, because she had a kid at home, usually meant her car, my car, in the office, hers, mine and just for spite, on Will's couch. My new found freedom of spur of the moment sex was definitely out of character for me, whether or not it was for her I didn't want to know. The truth is, besides what I learned about her and her family when we talked on the way to the 4ᵗʰ of July party, I didn't know nor did I want to know anything more about who she was or what she did before me. For me being with Jess was like I was trying to start all over, trying to learn from all of the times I had failed at love before and use those failures to make this one work. I had completely convinced myself that I just needed to care about the then and now. On the nights Amalee's useless father had custody, Jess and I would go down to Friar Tuck's Bar or Miss Kate's after work, drink on the cheap well into the evening and dance to Motown on the juke boxes and then try to find our way back to her place. It didn't take long for me to realize that her house was too far from the bars to navigate safely, mostly after I drove up onto someone's lawn (taking out about 20 feet of azalea bushes before hitting the brakes) while we were heading uptown at about three in the morning. Plus, I wanted a place closer to the office for our trysts, which pretty much happened daily. My house, at least as far as I was concerned was out of the question as I couldn't bear the thought of taking this pristine relationship inside of the place where so much of the anger and bitterness from my marriage still hung about the walls like old paper. So I acquired the rental house, owned by a friend of mine in a wacky little neighborhood called the Irish Channel.

Because of her joint custody we had relatively few Saturday nights out together, two, maybe three. Those were followed by lazy Sunday mornings with Jess dragging herself from the bedroom in back of the shotgun, through the kitchen to the thrift store sofa in the living room where she would stretch out on the broken and torn leather, wrap herself in my ancient letterman's blanket from high school, and lapse back into what I called her second sleep as I made coffee, breakfast and started Sunday dinner, usually a large cast iron pot of etouffe or gumbo made with leftovers from the week.

"I don't know what to tell you," she said, one balmy Sunday afternoon as we sat on my porch steps reading the Times-Picayune and drinking Abita beers, "I really, really like you and care about you a lot, but don't know if I can love you…"

"But…"

"…and I want to warn you not fall in love with me, I'm a mess."

I thought about what she said for a moment, then put my arm around her and kissed her on the forehead, "Honey, you are no more a mess than any of the rest of us. Everyone has problems, at least you try and deal with yours, some, like my ex-wife prefer just to lie to themselves, and lie to everyone else in order to hide from theirs."

"I lied to myself about Stephen. I told myself that he loved me even though he never said it himself."

"He didn't?"

"Nope."

"Well, what the hell…I lov…" and with that she quickly covered my lips with hers. When we parted she looked at me deeply and warned, "I told you not to say that."

"Ever?"

"Maybe not ever, but for certain not right now, and not in the immediate future"

"Okay, whatever you want."

I waited another whole week to ask her again about what it was she thought we had together. We were on a date, another real date that is, not just drinks and bed, and went to see a wonderful play, about Richard Feynman and how he dealt with his cancer diagnosis. During the second act as "Feynman" was talking with his oncologist about his cancer and lamenting over his womanizing, Jess leaned over to me and whispered "I'm going to hurt you, you know that don't you?"

"Right now?" I asked, hoping she was teasing me about later in bed, but somehow knew better.

"I'm serious Johnny."

"How can you be so sure?" The actor that played Feynman looked at us. I was sure he could hear us though no one nearby 'shushed' or said anything to us.

"I just am." She whispered. Her was voice soft and full of sadness as she turned toward the stage and reached for my hand. I was always perplexed when she would say things like that; things like "I'm going to hurt you" "I'm bad for you", "I don't deserve you", which she did often. I couldn't figure out how such a smart and beautiful woman could get such a skewed vision of herself. To me, it was simple, we fit, each part of her, emotionally, physically, her work, fit with mine, driven by an unspoken but fully realized mutual respect for each other as thoughtful caring people. There was no pretension, no inflated ego or lying; there was no need for it.

"What?" I said still half sleeping. We were laying in bed, having just woken up on a rainy Saturday morning about a week later. She was facing away from me, her butt pressed against my side, her impressive heat easily felt through my battered t-shirt that covered her like the tarp of a baseball field.

"I've been thinking about what you can call this, what we have between us, and I came up with kinda-sorta"

"Kinda-sorta is the best you can do?" I didn't look at her face,I didn't want to show my hurt.

"Yeah…" she rolled over and looked at me, her eyes closing slowly, then opening again, I couldn't tell if she was sleepy, or trying to think things out for herself.

"…It's like we're kinda-sorta dating, kinda-sorta in a relationship, but not quite."

"Is that your way of putting in an 'out' clause on us?"

"I'm just not ready Johnny, you treat me great, you care about me, but so help me god I'm not ready to commit to anything beyond this and I'm certainly not ready to fall in love."

I didn't want to force her into anything, but something deep wanted to know if it was me that kept her from doing this, kept her from opening her heart to me.

"It's just…" she sighed, put her head against my chest and began talking to the wall behind me. "…when Stephen broke up with me, I was shattered, beaten. Not physically, he never hit me…Well he never hit me hard, or anything…I was more like emotionally whipped. I just knew that I was worthless and unlovable and that I was the reason he left for someone else. I hated everything about me. Christ, I was so fucked up I even hated Amalee because she looked like me. That's when my parents stepped in and helped me out, took care of her for a while, paid my bills so I could try and get right again, and eventually I started to function, though I suppose the jury is still out as to whether or not I am 'right' or even functioning."

"I'm sorry Jess."

"Don't be."

"But…"

"And here you come," she interrupted, "you're nice, you're thoughtful and you listen to me, better than anyone has or should."

"Is it that bad?"

"No, just different, and it's something I am definitely not used to. I think it just will take some time." I held her close and we both stared off into some unknown distance. I looked at the water that was streaking down the window and played the game of seeing which drop would make it to the bottom of the sash first.

"I don't want to scare you off," I said.

"Same here,"

"You don't want me to scare you off?" I teased trying to lighten things up a bit.

"You know what I mean, asshole." She snarled lightly as she pinched me on my side. I laughed and slapped at her hands. We settled back in, quiet in our thoughts, neither of us in any hurry.

"You aren't bad for me." I say as I stroke her hair back from her forehead. She paused for a moment.

"Just wait." She answered.

Fifteen

———◆·❊·◆———

I LOVE A streak. Streaks mean things are happening, things are going on. Streaks can mean you're hot or you're cold, but you're something. And after beginning two of the last three days throwing my guts up, I am on a streak. Though there is a certain undeniable sense that perhaps things aren't quite working out the way you'd hoped with your life when you spend your first waking moments of the day being tossed about like a rag doll on the bathroom floor because your body is purging itself of alcohol. I'm not sure, but after years of study it's apparent that the purging occurs as a result of rejection. Not just the obvious physical rejection, but also perhaps a spiritual rejection as well. In the first instance, alcohol is, as much as I want to deny it, a foreign substance and depending on a person's constitution, the alcohol is rejected sooner or later. The spiritual rejection happens at the end of the evening, especially one spent stopping at every bar between my parents place in Bentwood and my house in New Orleans and hitting on every woman drawing breath that I met and still coming home alone. When the women who frequent bars on Sunday nights don't want you, trust me, you don't want you either. Hence, here I am, resting my face where others rest their ass and I'm not too proud to admit it feels good. The porcelain is cool to the touch and the little rim around the bowl is a perfect place to hold on to. And I can depend on it. After all, the toilet is here in my time of need. More than I can say about a lot of things in my life.

I attempt to think without moving my head and put the pieces of the night together as best I can. As near as I can remember, I got to bed somewhere around 5.30 this morning and set my alarm for 7.30, thinking I would need only a couple of hours of sleep before going to work. I was only off by ten or twelve. As I try to focus I see that all three of the watches on my right hand tell me that it is fast approaching 8 o'clock and I'm not sure that I'm done with the dry heaves. With great care and effort I manage to pull myself along the bathroom floor to the claw-footed tub and turn the water on as hot as I can stand it. Optimistic, I attempt to pull myself upright for the shower, but the best I can do is flop over the edge of the tub like a great walrus and lay in the bottom as the water scalds me crawfish red. I try to reassure myself that my behavior from the previous night was the result of the stress of dealing with my parents, but not currently in the mood to rationalize, force myself to cop to the truth that I have been acting like this since high school. But, wait a minute, this time, I had a right to act like a fucking idiot, I had a right to howl at the moon as a songwriter friend of mine likes to say. I used to be happy, Goddammit! Just a few weeks ago as a matter of fact, and now look at me! Of course that I was actually happy was probably the first sign that I should have known that something was going to foul things up. I was happy with work, I was very happy with Jess and hell, I was even happy with me. And that was a big deal. The Fourth of July party at Tim and Andy's was almost two years to the day since my divorce was finalized. Two years of trying to figure out who I was, and what I wanted, two years of de-toxifying myself from a relationship so poisonous that when my wife finally told me it was over, the sense of relief was such that I imagined myself strapped to the electric chair, the executioner's hand on the lever and ready to pull as the phone rings with the governor's reprieve, in Texas no less. Two years...was happy...am not happy...what the fuck is happy...this shower is burning my skin off...the thoughts run through my mind at an alarming rate...I pull myself up from the bottom of the tub, lean precariously over the edge and heave into the toilet bowl. It seems to last for a lifetime, but, finally I am empty.

I fall back into the tub sending water cascading over the edge. Thoughts of drowning myself are pushed back down into the haze and I finally try to motivate, but can barely stand as I reach to turn the shower off. Stumbling out, I lean against the sink, steadying myself with my right hand as I reach for a towel. I brush my teeth while sitting on the toilet lid and resting my forehead against the sink. By the time I dress and head to my car it is almost 9 o'clock and my plans for getting to the office before anyone else are fucked. I drive carefully, hands at 10 and 2, sweating profusely and aiming the car for the middle on of the three streets I see through eyes that have so much blood in them, "stained" falls way short of description. The city falls away in soft focus as I drive, landmarks I have known since childhood become a blur of Crayola colors. My head pounds like the drums of a Robert Bly outing as I park my car and walk thunderous steps into the office.

Jess is here. I don't mean here as in she's somewhere in the building and I sense some "disturbance in the force" here. She's right fucking here in front of me as I open the door. No time to plan, no time to come up with something witty to say, no time to do jack shit. Just enough time to look through the haze of no sleep and enough alcohol in my bloodstream to choke a goat and see her talking with one of our agency producers, feel my heart start racing so fast my pulse had to be visible in my forehead, gasp in surprise and shuffle off to my office like a scolded child. I close the door behind me and lock it, lean against it, place my head into my hands and not knowing what else to do I begin crying. For the first time in my life I am at a loss. I am filled with such…I don't know what I am filled with. My mother lies deathly ill in a hospital and for all I know she is sinking away right now and I am not sure that I could raise one ounce of feeling toward her one way or the other. But seeing Jess, knowing that she has apparently made a definitive choice in her life to exclude me, somehow makes the loss of her, for the first time, tangible. I walk over to the small closet that I use to keep my filing cabinet in, by way of trying to make my office look less like an office. True to the hardboiled stereotype, I open the bottom drawer and pull out a bottle of Jameson's Whiskey. I take two quick shots and it hits me like a punch in the gut, and my first response is to gag and throw it back up. But I fight the urge, determined to hold it down, and to prove to no one in particular, my sense of manhood…I force feed myself another shot.

A timid, very quick knock on my office door persuades me to cap the bottle and replace it quietly. I've never considered myself an alcoholic, which of course is the first indication that I am one, but have no time to debate the three shots I've just had at nine thirty in the morning, as the knock repeats, firmer this time.

"I'm on the phone." I call out.

"No you're not." Fuck, it's Jess and I do not, under any circumstance want to talk to her. I'm in no fucking mood and I certainly don't want to hear what she has to say, so I pick up the phone and start dialing, my father of all people.

"I am now!" I shout back at the door.

"We have to talk, John, at some point we have to talk. You haven't said a half dozen words to me in a month."

My father's phone starts ringing but he doesn't pick up.

"Why start now?" I shout back turning back to the file cabinet and the Jameson's, I've had three, a fourth can only help right? Though I am starting to sweat a bit on my forehead and my chest is pounding so hard I can feel my pulse in my eyeballs.

"Please?" she calls in a plaintive voice. I hate it when she humbles herself, it doesn't suit her. *Come on Dad pick up the fucking phone!*

"Not now Jess, my mother went back into the hospital this weekend..." she knows Mother is in and out of the hospital so I flavor the excuse, "... and they say it doesn't look good." As the words leave my lips, the sound of them hangs in the air and for the first time I actually hear them. I feel a bit guilty, both for not recognizing the severity of Dr. Harris' words yesterday and for using my mother's condition to get rid of Jess. It passes. I give in to the whiskey that calls from the cabinet.

"I'm sorry", she says, more humble than before, "Maybe later..."

I hear her walk away. My parent's automated message comes on; I hang up without leaving a message of my own, sit down and re-open the bottle.

My phone rings less than five minutes later, I stare at the phone and figure it to be Jess trying to circumvent the locked door. Instead, it's my father, "Sorry I didn't pick it up when you called, John, but I was on the phone with Mother's social worker". The words 'Mother's social worker' mixed with the whiskey immediately have me imagining my mother as an indigent, lying in her own filth, on a shitty bed in a crowded ward on some forgotten floor of the massive Charity Hospital that serves as the main source of health care for the poor of New Orleans. Chronic overcrowding and unconscionably under funded, the only bright spot in Charity's otherwise dismal sky is that because of the high rate of violence in the city, Charity's emergency room is the training ground for some of the best ER physicians in the country.

My father continues talking, unaware of the mental side trip that I have taken thanks to the whiskey. "She says the best thing for Mother may be a stay in the hospital's rehab facility until we can figure out where to send her for the long term."

"What long term? Didn't Dr. Harris say that he doesn't expect her to make the end of the year?"

"That's only his opinion John, he could be wrong you know, and I can't take of mother by myself any more. Of course..."

"Of course, what Dad?" *Something's coming I can sense it.*

"If you could help out then maybe she could come home."

"I do help out, I come out on the weekends, I buy groceries, I buy beer..."

"You know what I mean Johnny, you could close up your house for a while and come out to Bentwood. Your mother would appreciate it. I would appreciate it."

"I'm not doing anything to my house…"

"Why not?"

"Because I work in the city, the commute alone would take three hours out of every day and besides, how could I help?"

"You could help by being there for your mother."

"By what!?" I almost laugh out loud. It is when moments like this occur that a prudent person would tell my father that they would call him back, hang up the phone and waited a day or so before talking to him again. But the four shots have taken a firm hold and any thoughts of being prudent are well drowned in Irish whiskey.

"When was she ever *there* for me?"

"Johnny, I don't want to hear this, not here, not now!"

"Maybe you do need to hear this, maybe you need to hear how she treated me!"

"She was a good mother!"

"Yeah Pop, she did the things a mother was supposed to do and to Harry, yeah, she was a good mother. But the truth is she treated me like shit. So, if she needs somebody to 'be there' for her then maybe she should have a séance and see if that useless bastard brother of mine will show up, but you know what? I bet he doesn't, he didn't in life and he sure as shit ain't doin' it in death!"

The line was dead. I don't know when he hung up, but he did and I would have to apologize. But not yet, damn it. I want to be mad, and I want to hate. I want to hate Mother, I want to hate Harry, and I want to hate Jess. I want to hate the whole goddamn world, and I've wanted to hate it all since I was thirteen years old but the goddamn church told me I shouldn't. The church told me I had to turn the other cheek, I had to forgive, I had to let things go, but the goddamn church didn't have to sit by while I busted my ass to get straight A's and still got ignored while Harry barely passed and got praised when he got a C. The church wasn't there when I was the one who cooked for Harry and my father on the days Mother worked, or when I was the one who cleaned both of our rooms because Harry had to be allowed to "find himself".

And find himself he did, what he found was that he didn't want to do jack shit. No, it wasn't even that he didn't want to do it,it was that he shouldn't have had to do anything. Harry wanted everything handed to him, and everything was, including Mother's love. Stephen wants it handed to him and he gets Jess' love. I busted my ass, I was there for the holidays, and I was there with groceries, booze and money. I was there when Jess needed to know that she could be loved and was loved, and where am I now?

By my fucking self.

Good guys finish last, Mr. Durocher? How about this as a corollary to your rule? How about good guys get the shit kicked out of them and end up in the ditch…sounds better to me. Mother wants me there?

Fat fucking chance, you get what you give honey.

Sixteen

EVERYTHING BECAME UNRAVELED over a phone call. Or more directly, everything became unraveled over the lack of a phone call. Jess and I had "come out of the closet" to a couple of our closest co-workers, (who, we found out, had had their suspicions anyway) and we had been invited to a birthday party where we would have exposed our relationship to the rest of those at J. Thomas Hunt, including Will, and one of the New York creative directors. I was excited because I was sick of the slinking around and wanted a sense of legitimacy. Jess and I often fantasized about what the reaction would be when our co-workers, especially Will, found out about us. The weekend of the party was Jess' weekend to have Amalee. She had arranged for a baby-sitter for the Saturday night soirée, but wanted to spend Friday with her daughter. A couple of us from the office were headed out to the movies, three or four all told, including me. That the rest of those going were women wasn't a concern for either Jess or myself, because they were women we had both been working with for a while, one of them knew about our relationship, and Jess knew there was nothing that was going to happen between any of them and myself. At least I thought she knew that. The last really civil conversation occurred as I stood outside of the movie theatre waiting for everyone to show up. I remember it ended with her saying she would call me later, as she remembered it, I said I would call. Of course, neither of us called that night. It was the following afternoon when I finally called her to talk about picking her up for the party..

"Hey!"

"Hey…let me call you in a few minutes, I'm watching a movie…"

"Yeah…sure," She never, ever blew me off for television, not without at least a short, somewhat disjointed explanation of what she was watching and why.

An hour and a half later I finally got tired of waiting and called her back.

"Hey, what's up? I thought you were going to call me back?"

"And I thought you were going to call last night." For the first time since I had known her; dating, not dating, whatever the hell you wanted to call it, Jess seemed angry with me. No, I take that back, she didn't **seem** angry, she was angry. I replied in a fashion typical for the average stupid man.

"I thought you were going to call, so we're even. Did you have fun with…"

"I can't do this."

"Can't do what?"

"This…I can't see you any more."

And there it was. Now, I was a baseball player as a kid, in high school and in college. But, I still do not know how the expression that something unexpected has come "out of left field" ever became a part of the lexicon. And using it here seems so inadequate that were I to place a more appropriate metaphor using direction, distance and a baseball field for reference, say Shea Stadium, then forget left field, this came out of fucking Quebec. I held onto the phone, my heart in my throat and looked around my kitchen for the portable defibrillator I knew I should have bought when I was still married.

"Why? Just because I didn't call you? But I really thought you were going to call me!"

"Look…" she says, I heard her voice quiver, "It's not about the phone call, but how I felt when I didn't get the phone call."

"What do you mean?"

"Stephen would go out, sometimes for hours on end, and I wouldn't hear anything. I would lie awake knowing that he was fucking someone else. I would go back and forth between seething with anger and jealousy, and just wanting to hear that he wasn't dead. When I didn't hear from you last night, I fell back into that old pattern and got jealous. The feeling reminded me too much of what it was like to be with him."

"Jealous? Shit Jess, you knew who I was with and what I was doing. More importantly you know how I feel about you."

"I know, that's what's so hard. You are so nice, and treat me better than any man has since my grandfather; I fought with myself, argued with myself, told myself that I don't deserve you. Maybe I don't, maybe I do…I just think, that because of last night, because of the thoughts that I had, I'm just not ready for this."

I stood there with the phone against my face, not wanting to hang up, wanting only to find some way to change her mind, to let her know just how much I loved her, more than any other woman I had ever met in my life. I wanted some physical symbol, some kind of massive display like the Taj Mahal that said 'Hey! Woman! See here? See how great and tall and big this is? It stretches from the ground to forever. Don't believe me? Then see for yourself. This is me! This is my love for you, from here to forever!'...Instead I said only the words I have ever regretted in my whole life.

"What ever you want." And hung the phone up.

I looked at a magnetic calendar with a painting of Rodrigue's 'Blue Dog' sitting in the shade of a large oak tree that was holding fast to the front of my refrigerator, the date was August 14th. I couldn't believe that it didn't even have the decency to end with some sort of catastrophic flair. I figured that when someone feels this strongly for someone else there at least should be some drama with the end of it. Murder-suicide maybe, at least a screaming confrontation over dinner in a fancy restaurant, throwing the drink in the face sort of thing, but no, not me, Christ, I couldn't even end a relationship decently. The great love of my life had lasted all of six weeks and when I left the house to go get a drink, it was like it hadn't even happened at all.

Seventeen

I TAKE A big deep breath and emerge from my office expecting to see the face of each and every employee of J. Thomas Hunt waiting for me, instead the office is as it should be; Will is tucked away looking at porn and in general hoping no one bothers him. The edit suite doors are closed, presumably with work going on behind them. Everyone else is out on the front porch smoking. That is truly one of the great things about our society today, we are all so scared; of what, I don't know, nothing…everything…I don't even think we know, but we're scared, so much so that we don't really care about anyone else. I could've shown up today, smuggled a pistol in with my un-used laptop, locked my door and blown a hole in my head the size of a Zulu coconut and no one would have noticed until the smell behind the door began to ruin their appetites. After discovering my badly decaying body, they would climb over each other in an effort to see who would take possession of my corner space.

I walk over to the edit suites and slowly open the door. Inside I hear the familiar voice of Aussie Bob, my co-conspirator in the great 4th of July revolt. He waves me in and I take the seat next to him. He hangs up the phone and turns to me, "Jess was looking for you."

"Yeah, I know, she came to my office."

"Have you been out drinking?"

"A bit last night, why?"

"You take a shower any time lately?" Bob has turned his attention to the commercial video on the computer screens of the editing system. His hands work the keyboard like Doctor John playing some of Professor Longhair's infamous Shufflin' Hungarian on the piano, and he makes swift changes to the video I see on the screens.

"Do I smell?" I ask, but before he can answer I jump into the edit, "I don't want the dog in that shot…"

"Bloody hell, you smell and the dog has to be in the shot because he is in every bloody take of that shot." Bob doesn't look away from the screen and keeps playing the silent keyboard.

"I ate some Certs."

"It ain't your breath mate, it's your whole body, you must be oozing the stuff. I can barely stand sittin' next to you." He whips his hands across the keys, selects more footage from one of the hard drives, and pulls up a shot without the dog.

"I told you", I say smelling my shirt, he's right, I stink. I smell like stale beer.

"Well I like the dog anyway." Bob is getting snarky with me, he like most editors enjoy working alone.

"So keep the damn dog."

"Why are you in here anyway? You hate being in here."

"I'm hiding." I turn and look back at the closed door

"From Jess…?"

"Exactly…"

"Why?"

"Because Bob…just because I don't want to see her right now." The anger begins to surface again, both because I don't want to talk about Jess and because I am sitting in the edit suite. Bob is right, I hate it in here. I hate the whole process of editing. Mostly because it is the point in which everyone else involved in the commercial sees what I've shot and immediately becomes a critic and always has a better idea of what to do. Never mind that I make my clients a bunch of money, never mind that I'm the one that puts in the time.

"You and Jess have something going on?" Bob shakes me out of my second hate rant in fifteen minutes.

"What?"

"I said do you and Jess have something going on?"

"Had something…" I take a breath, what the hell, she's re-married or what ever so there no sense in keeping it quiet anymore plus with Bob I'm thinking I can get a guy-to-guy bitch session going. "We had something, for a couple of months."

"Oh…"

I wait…and wait, "That's it?"

"You like this here?"

Bob has rearranged some things on the edit, to be honest I could care less, but I lie, "Yeah that's great." He goes back to work. I can't let this go, this is earth-shattering news I am giving him, I am opening up my soul, I am letting him know that Jess and I had a torrid inter-office 'affair de coeur', big time gossipy stuff.

"Is 'oh' all you can say?"

"About what?" Jesus Christ, what a dolt. Its no wonder only about ten percent of the fucking Australian continent is populated, who wants to live on a fucking island surrounded by people who are so out of touch?

"About me and Jess! Is that all you can say about us?"

"What the hell else should I say? You are two adults, or at least one of you are with her being the one, so what should I say?" He has stopped working and looks irritated.

He's right. What's the big deal? We are two adults, we had our shot, it didn't work out. I'm reasonably handsome, fat but handsome, I'm mostly witty and I have a cool job. Well, at least other people think it's cool, I find it trite and the business filled with people I wouldn't piss on if they were on fire, unless I could piss gas as the saying goes. So what is the big deal? Yeah.

The door opens and Jess sticks her head in. "Can we talk?"

"Not now, I'm busy." I say curtly. She pauses as if she wants to say something, and then slowly backs out of the door, closing it lightly.

An uncomfortable moment passes between Bob and I, until he stops his frantic manipulation of the keyboard and slowly turns to me.

"So…how serious were you two?"

I thought I had waited until everyone had left before poking my head out of my office at the end of the day, but she was there, waiting.

"I want to talk to you, Johnny and I am not going to let this wait another day. I'll follow you home, I'll break your door down, whatever but we have to get some things straight between us. There are some things you need to hear."

"Fine. Let's talk."

"Not here."

"Okay Jess, wherever you want to go. I take a nice dramatic pause as she picks up her backpack. "How late will your husband let you stay out?" Sometimes I think I corner the market in childish.

She gave a look through the top of her eyes that I used to love, "He took Amalee to dinner at his momma's, and they won't be home for a couple of hours, nine-thirty or ten."

"Okay, so what do you want to do?"

"I'm hungry, let's go get something to eat." This is exactly what I don't want, doing anything with her that will con me into thinking there some sort of normalcy between us, anything that will tell me that we are just two people going to dinner, or worse that I begin diluting myself that we could in any way get back together.

"Fine, just pick a place and I'll meet you there." *Good. Short, to the point, don't give in to her...*

"You don't want to ride together?"

"Jesus Christ, Jess! No, I don't want to ride together" *What the hell is she doing to me? Is she so fucking blind...?"*

"You hate me." *No, I love you, you jackass.*

"I don't hate you Jess, and you're instigating, so do you want to talk here or go eat?"

"Fine, I'll meet you at Bart's." She turns and starts to leave.

"Fine..."

She turns back and looks at me for a moment then stumbles out of the door, falling over some empty cardboard boxes stacked for the cleaning people and into one of the walls of the narrow foyer. I smile, the woman is a klutz without twenty pounds of crap on her back, and with the extra weight she's a menace to society.

Bart's is a neighborhood joint and my favorite restaurant in a city full to the edges with restaurants. Located up Canal Street about fifteen minutes from downtown in an area of New Orleans called Mid-City, Bart's offers the typical neighborhood food; fried seafood, trout almandine, gumbo, turtle soup, poor boys and Italian dishes like spaghetti and meatballs or veal parmesan among others. My personal favorites are 'crab fingers', which are the pincher part of the crab claw, with the meat on the claw still attached. They are first coated in Italian breadcrumbs, then broiled in garlic and butter, and served with toasted French bread so that you can "sop" up the sauce. I then have the half and half poor boy, which is half fried shrimp and half fried oysters. Dressed with lettuce, tomato, mayonnaise and pickles, of course. And finally, bread pudding with a hot rum sauce. I would kill for less. There are no reservations at Bart's, you walk into the restaurant through the screen door, which opens to a side street and stands a couple of feet from the end of the bar. When you get in, if you can get in, on Fridays and Saturdays the place is jammed, you give your name to the bartender, the number of people in your party, he takes your name, your drink order and you wait. This is the policy for everyone, regardless of who you are except for perhaps prominent local musicians, politicians (especially assessors), police or the health department. Basically, it's the policy for everyone except for those that can shut Bart's down on a whim. I get there before Jess and give the bartender my name and tell her that there are two of us. She says of course, that the wait is twenty minutes, Jess walks in as I buy two beers, I slide one of the beers in front of her, lean against the bar and with my best Bogart, "Of all the gin joints in all the world, why did she have to pick mine?"

"Very nice." She says, "Woody Allen?"

"Very funny, the bartender says we have the standard twenty minutes until the table is ready. You want to talk now or wait until we sit to tear my heart out"

"I'll wait until we sit thank you, that way I can make it last longer."

"Ouch...callous wench."

It was more like ten minutes for the table. To be honest, I would have been happy just to stay there at the bar, there was a closer proximity to alcohol and if we weren't going to talk until we sat then maybe we wouldn't have to talk at all. Our waiter, an earnest and hurried young black man sat us, got our drink and crab finger order and quickly turned away to put it in before heading to a table of eight college students, (from the self important and somewhat vacant looks on their faces I'm betting they attend Tulane) that sat at the same time as we did, the mark of good service. I held the menu high enough to cover my face in order to avoid looking and talking to Jess. It didn't work.

"Put that down, you already know what you're getting."

"What do you mean?"

"You're getting the shrimp and oyster sandwich."

"Noooo...well maybe...damn...am I that predictable?"

"Absolutely..."

I place the menu on the table as the waiter brings our drinks. She has stayed with beer while I have moved on to Jack Daniels and diet Coke, just something to wet my whistle, and it is only Monday after all. "So?" What the hell, I might as well get this started.

"So..." Jess takes a deep breath, a sip of her beer and looks at me with those damn eyes. "So what have you heard?"

"About what...?"

"Don't be an asshole."

"I heard that you and Stephen took off for Vegas and got married over the weekend."

"You did?"

"Oh, and I heard you paid for it." The waiter has returned with our crab fingers and is waiting for our dinner order; he looks over at the table of college kids, which is growing increasingly louder and appears to be on the verge of full-blown college asshole rowdiness and curses at them under his breath. He is around their age, grew up in this city and works for a living. They are modern society's equivalent of Reconstruction carpetbaggers ending up in New Orleans and at Tulane because of footage of girls showing their tits in the

French Quarter and the fact that they couldn't get into one of the Ivy League schools in spite of their alumni parents. They are largely from the Northeast, spend their parents' money on drugs, and fraternity keggers on Frat House row. They fight over frigid girlfriends named Kat or Winnie who are only in school to get their "MRS" degree. And worst of all they treat locals like they are servants and throw up in the street during Mardi Gras...if you can't tell yet, I'm on the waiter's side.

Jess orders the trout, I of course, order the poor boy and another drink, and damn these glasses are small, I mean, how much liquor can the possibly put in them? I dive into the crab fingers, picking a fat one up by the end of the pointed hard shell, rub it in the butter and garlic sauce and jam it into my mouth. I can actually hear my cholesterol rising. The best and most efficient way to eat crab fingers is to place the meat end, (dripping with garlic and butter sauce) in your mouth, while holding just the tip of the claw. Close your mouth until your teeth are just about to touch, then pull the claw out, using your teeth to scrape the meat off of the claw. About a dozen come to the order and depending on how hungry I am, I might only be able to manage three or four orders. This being a Monday, and not the busiest night of the week for Bart's, our claws came out rather quickly and much to my surprise when I bite down on the claw, find it to be only slightly less hot than if I had placed my tongue on a stove burner.

"Owww fuck!" I drop the remainder of the claw onto the appetizer plate and chug what is left of my drink.

"You burn your mouth?" Jess smiles as she takes a claw and blows on it to cool it.

"No, it's a new tradition I've started with every meal. My mother really loves it."

She laughs, "I've really wanted to try these but the grease scares me" and carefully takes a bite.

"It's not grease it's butter, there's a difference." I have forgotten how nice it is to share a meal with someone.

"Not much of one." She takes the crab claw slowly out of her mouth, I try not to focus on how sexy her lips are, "Ow, fuck" she says and takes a big sip finishing her beer. I turn, find the waiter and using the silent hand universal "thirsty" hand signal, point at Jess and make the drinking motion.

"How are you?" She says.

"Fine..." I hope the response bothers her.

"Your mom not doing well?"

"No." *She's gonna drop dead and I don't care because you left me.*

"Why is this so hard?"

"What, are you kidding me? Why is this so hard? If I have to tell you that then this conversation is a waste of your time and mine." *Where the fuck is my drink?*

"That's not what I meant."

"Then what did you mean?"

"It's been two months since we dated John, can't we just be…"

"Be what? Friends!?" I begin hyperventilating and turn to actively search for our waiter, if I see him fucking with those college kids I'm gonna get my drink myself.

"Keep your voice down!" Jess reaches out and grabs my hand. The waiter appears with both of our drinks, he serves her first then places mine in front of me. I take a big gulp and down half of it. "You might as well get me another; this'll be gone by the time you get back."

"Oh, that's nice, get drunk, that'll help."

"Maybe not you, but it'll make me feel a whole lot better."

We quiet down for a few moments, I eat some more of the crab claws, while she absently drinks her beer and nibbles at the French bread that sits in the basket at her elbow. I am beginning to catch my breath again.

"Dip the bread in the butter sauce." She looks at me, a small smile appears and she takes a piece of the bread and rubs the bottom of the plate with it. The bread emerges covered in butter and garlic and loose bread crumbs from the claws and Jess takes a bite, "Oh my God…" she savors the bread as she chews, her eyes closed, and her breath heavy. There may be better things to put in your mouth, but I am hard pressed to come up with suggestions.

"Better than sex, right?"

"Actually…yes." She smiles. I take a piece of the bread and do the same.

"Yes Johnny."

"Yes, Johnny what?"

"I want us to be friends. We have to work together, can't we just get along there?"

"We get along fine."

"You don't talk to me, even when we have a project together, and when you see me you give me these looks."

"What looks?" *Other than the ones where I try and use telepathy to enter into your body, find your heart and tear it as if it were a sheet of paper, taking my thumb and forefinger and ripping it into strips, slowly, deliberately over the course of ten or maybe twenty years. Oh, you mean those looks?*

"You know what looks…"

"No, really, I don't"

"The ones you give when we pass in the hall, the ones that say that you hate me."

"I don't hate you." *Oh what the hell, let's just get it out, no sense dancing around the real issue,* "Are you really married?" I blurt. Jess takes a sip of her beer; she holds the bottle in from of her mouth, her eyes dance back and forth as she contemplates,

"You mean legally?"

"Yes legally, what the hell does that mean?"

"Stephen has moved back in, and we are trying to make it work, and yes we went to Vegas for the weekend, but no, we didn't get married." My heart leaps, no marriage for her may mean there is still hope for me, the only thing I can do now is lie convincingly;

"That's good to hear. I really wish the best for you, if it's Stephen, then it's Stephen."

"You don't mean that." *Damn, she knows me well.*

"Yes I do, I want the best for you, and for Amalee." *The best meaning "me" of course, how can that ass wipe compare to me?*

"So do I Johnny and that means I give him a chance to prove himself to me, that he loves me and can commit to me"

Jesus lady, you really want this guy to fail don't you? I mean, there's no way in hell he'll be able to do all of that, once an asshole always an asshole I always say. I'm laying even money that he cheats on you again in six months, and when he does if you think you can just come and knock on my door and expect me to pick up the pieces, well, then you're absolutely right.

"Do you think he'll be able to do it?"

"I hope so. But, I have to try Johnny, he's been calling me a lot and saying all the right things, you know…I guess I just have to see for myself. I have to make sure I do everything right, so that if it doesn't work now…"

"Then you can't blame yourself, like you did the first time?"

"Yeah, I suppose I just need to know that, and I need to know that you and I can get along."

I pause, I don't want her to think that it's going to be this easy for us to get along, if it means so much to her then I want her sitting on the edge for a minute, and I am a nice guy right? Right?

"Of course we can get along, I'm sorry for the looks, it was just hard sometimes you know?"

"I know."

The waiter brings our drinks and another server brings the food right behind. I hold my fresh drink up to Jess, "Here's wishing you happiness and love…"

She touches her beer bottle to my glass, "And here's to friends."

"To friends" I say looking her in the eye, she smiles and we both take a self-congratulatory sip of our drinks. I stare at my plate for a moment and think about how terribly grown up I must seem on the surface and wonder if

I'll ever be able to actually live up to that facade. I look up at her as she takes a bite and wonder why I love her so much, why her of all of the women I have known. The talk between us ends here and we eat our dinner surrounded by noise, but awash in our own uncomfortable silence.

Eighteen

"Strained". That's the word I've been searching for, as I sit smoking a cigarette on what has become my father's bench outside of the rehabilitation facility. Mother has been placed here only temporarily, either until she can go home or until they can find an even more depressing place to put her, if that is possible. I think of that word as in things have not always been strained between my mother and myself, in fact, were someone to have come up to me before Harry became such a selfish asshole, I would have said something to the effect of having been brought up in a very Ozzie and Harriet type of household. My childhood memories revolve around coming home from school to home baked cookies, (my mother, in spite of her diabetes, because of it, or both, refused to temper her love for baked goods, a love I inherited); diet soda, which back then was either Fresca or Tab, and sitting with Harry on the den floor and watching reruns of the Three Stooges. We were just kids then, born late to my folks who were thirty-nine when Harry showed up and forty-three when I arrived. I know for a fact that Mother had at least one miscarriage before we showed up. After that, she either had trouble getting pregnant, they decided to wait, or more likely we were big fat surprises.

We went to neighborhood public schools, something unheard of for white people in New Orleans today. Our parents dropped us off at McDonough #39 Elementary on St. Roch Avenue in the mornings and Harry and I would walk home every afternoon, unless it was storming, then we would get picked up. Harry and I did things together back then. After school usually meant hooking up with friends and playing baseball in the vacant lot at the end of the block behind Joey Bartels' house with Joey and his three bothers and whoever else we could get from our end of the street. There was a big family that lived midway down the street from us, the Kennedy's. Irish Catholic from head to toe, they had three boys and three girls, and there were always two or three of them up for whatever was going on. There were Friday night games of "Kick the Can" that would've lasted all night if Stacey Bourgeois the youngest of our next door neighbors, hadn't felt the need to quit every time she was told that she was "it". And there was hanging out down at the "Rocks", a line of old growth oak trees that marked the entrance of our subdivision from Elysian Fields Avenue and was surrounded by a low brick wall. Within the brick wall some sick, twisted, obviously childless landscape architect had decided to dump countless thousands of the best throwing rocks anyone had ever seen, not thinking that idiot kids like ourselves would actually pick the rocks up, hide behind the trees and throw them at each other. Which of course we did on a daily basis. Not all of our activities as kids were without merit however. One chilly February afternoon, Harry, Joey Bartels and I were wandering the neighborhood looking for something to blow up with a couple of left over Black Cat firecrackers from New Years that Harry had found in a pair of pants that he forgot to put into the wash. We ended up back at Joey's house in the side yard surveying a large pile of crap that his German Shepard Rommel had deposited under the Bartels' kitchen window. It was Joey's job to clean up after the dog and Harry suggested planting the firecrackers into the pile of crap as a way of having one less pile for Joey to pick up. The resulting explosion covered the entire side of the Bartels' house, including the kitchen window, (where Joey's mom stood at the sink doing dishes) with dog shit. Needless to say, we spent the rest of the afternoon cleaning the outside of the whole house with a hose and brushes and complaining to Mrs. Bartels that we were close to succumbing to frostbite. Typical kids getting into typical trouble and back then Harry was a part of everything.

As we grew up, we grew apart. A lot of it was natural, given the age difference, a lot of it was Harry deciding along the way that he didn't want to be a part of the family anymore. This really became clear when he left New Orleans for college. After that we would see him on the odd Christmas vacation or maybe if my parents got up the nerve to drive and visit him during the summer. For the most part and for the rest of his time on the planet, to Mother, Father and I, Harry became a once a month voice on the phone. Mother took it the hardest of course, blaming herself for "letting him get away" when he went to school and blaming herself again when he got sick, and again finally when he died. My father, unaccustomed to dealing with so much feeling or emotion, was as left out of Mother's life as I was after Harry died, except that it was my father who had to take care of her once she started to refuse to do anything for herself. What is the most remarkable to me as I sit here on this bench on a lovely fall day doing nothing in particular but smoking cigarettes and waiting for Mother to die, is the speed with which things became unraveled once Harry went. It was if a starter pistol went off at his service and my mother was the only one in the blocks.

"You can come in and see her now, the respiratory therapist is done." My dad has stuck his head out of the front door of the facility. I get up, toss my cigarette on the ground and snuff it out with the heel of my shoe; turn to go in and thinking twice turn back, pick up the butt and toss it in the garbage.

"What'd you do that for?"

"I don't want to litter."

"They got people to pick that up; you're costing somebody a job."

"That's a good attitude dad."

"That's the truth Johnny, we start doing all the little jobs and people are going to be out of work, it's just like those self check out lines at the grocery store."

"What ever you say."

My father holds the door for me as I walk into the facility. A squat one-story wagon wheel shaped building that sits a hundred yards or so behind the main building of the hospital. At the interior hub of the wagon wheel, what I suppose can be considered the lobby of the place, is a semi circle desk that serves as the nurse's station. Patients in wheel chairs sit parked around the lobby; some are waiting to be taken into various rooms for their various therapies, while others just sit, looking lost, alone and confused. Their Kleenex- thin white robes hang about their bodies, exposing their grimy, too long lived-in pajamas. One black man sleeps in his wheel chair, his head hanging down, his shoulders slumped, his breath sounding like the nasal wheeze of an English Bulldog. Below his waist, the stump of a right leg juts out from beneath his robe; a crusty yellowing bandage covers the skin where his knee used to be. Rehab has the same antiseptic scent as the hospital, but also has the funky smell of sweat mixed in. We turn right at the desk and walk down a short hall with only four rooms. My father turns to me while we're still in the hall, "Here's the room John, I'm going to go in for a minute with you but then I'm going to run out to the Jiffy Mart and get some cigarettes and a couple of tickets for the lottery."

"You what...?" but before I can protest my father has the door open and is pushing me into Mother's room.

Just like the hospital, the rooms here in the rehab facility are cold (both literally and figuratively), with dingy gray walls, bad fluorescent lighting, a couple of uncomfortable, very ugly chairs and two beds. Mother is lying on top of her covers in the bed furthest from the door and nearest to the window, with a lovely view of the rear parking lot complete with a large blue and white dumpster that looks like it hasn't been emptied since the Johnson administration. A large black woman occupies the bed near the door and sleeps on her back, her large breast sagging down her sides almost touching the mattress and snoring loud enough to cause us to raise our voices to be heard. I look out the window at the dumpster for a moment fighting the urge to laugh out loud. Mother is not wearing a hospital gown, but is dressed in her own clothes; a pair of old, brown, stretch pants and a pink long sleeve top. She is wearing a white ankle sock on her left foot; her right is still covered by the adjustable air cast that they put on her when she got to the hospital last week. Her hair is drastically shorter, a result of a visit by the stylist the hospital sends around to long-term care patients who, like mother, for the most part could care less what they look like. Her complexion has waned to a shade lighter than tracing paper and only slightly less transparent. She has an oxygen tube affixed to her nostrils that trails down the side of the bed to the green cylinder that has become an extension of her lungs. And, to add a little touch of home to her surroundings she has carefully placed a four by six framed photo of a smiling Harry on her bedside table.

"Hello Mother." I say as I walk past snoring beauty to the side of her bed and kiss her on the forehead. Her skin feels clammy, cold and as if it is slowly pulling away from her forehead

"Why is it the weekend already? It must be because I think they must close the bridges between here and New Orleans during the week." The sarcasm drips so heavily from her mouth I expect to see it form a puddle on her shirt next to whatever she had for breakfast. Oatmeal?

I straighten up stiffly, decide quickly that I don't want to get embroiled with her quite so soon and walk over to a chair on the other side of the bed. "It's good to see you too, mother."

"Did you bring my shrimp sandwich?"

"No ma'am, I was told you couldn't eat fried foods any more."

"Who the hell said that?"

"Dr. Harris."

"I'm eighty-three years old I can eat whatever the hell I want."

"Evidently not."

"I'll talk to him."

"I bet you will."

My father, who has managed to stay out of the exchange, has one foot in the hall and the other pressed against the door, like a sprinter in the blocks. "I'll be right back Mother."

"Where are you going?" My mother rises up on her elbows to look at my father. I may be out of my mind but I actually think I hear for the first time in my life, fear in *her* voice. Is she afraid that he is leaving or is she afraid that he is leaving her alone with me?

"I'm just running out for cigarettes, I'll be right back."

She lays back down and looks away from him, "Go to Sonny's and get me a sandwich."

"You can't eat that and besides they're bringing you lunch in just a while. I'll be right back." And with that he disappeared faster than David Blaine on crystal meth. After hearing the door ease closed, Mother turned and looked at me.

"What?" I am defensive, but can't help it, it's as natural as breathing around her.

She sighs heavily…"I hate this place."

"Well, do the things they say, get better and go home." I look at my watch, *how long as he been gone? 30 seconds?*

"I don't want to go home either, your father is sick of taking care of me. I'm tired, John; I'm tired of the tubes, I'm tired of lying in bed and I'm tired of being sick. I feel like I've been sick my whole life." I look at her as she stares absently at her television, the volume down too low for anyone to hear. She looks tired, but she seems so aware. I try and remember if she was ever this morose when I was a kid or even after I had grown up.

"What do you want Mother?"

"I want an ice cream sundae. I want to walk without having to lean on something or someone; I want to be able to get through a day without taking a hat full of pills or a syringe full of pig serum. I want to wake up and look out of the window and not feel like I am looking at the world through a television screen, merely an observer and no longer a participant."

I am at a loss for what to say. My mother has not been this honest with me in years and the depth of her confession just now has me confronting an odd feeling. As I take an emotional step away from myself and look deeply into how what she has just said affected me, I suddenly recognize the odd feeling I'm having as sympathy. I have spent so much of the last five years creating a great wall of anger towards her and my brother that I have forgotten, at least where she is concerned, what it is like to be sympathetic. Homeless on the streets of New Orleans got my sympathy. Co-worker whose pet has just died? I feel bad for you. Nameless faceless dead due to war, famine and pestilence on a continent I have never been to and don't plan on ever going to? Not only do you get my sympathy, but my money too. But my mother, father, brother? Hell no. Why? Because…because…Come on now fella, time for a little of your own medicine, a little 'man in the mirror' never hurt anybody. Because it's easier to feel bad for someone you know by only the slimmest of circumstances? Yep. Because the people closest to you are held to higher degrees of need based on whatever it was that they last did for you? Right. So let me get this straight, if your mother's story were on page forty-three of the New York Times you would feel bad for her but because you've been here for the whole telling, because you feel wronged because of how you perceive she treated your brother, well then to her it's tough shit. Okay then, let me think about this for a moment. What we're saying is here, is that maybe I was wrong. Maybe?

As I was ready to concede to myself a grievous error in judgment in how I've dealt with my mother, she turns to me and in a clear loud voice says, "See if you can get the fat black broad to turn over or something, that snoring is driving me insane."

"I can't mother, just ignore it."

"Ignore it hell, it's like trying to ignore a goddamn freight train rolling through the room." I get up from the chair and walk to the door. "Where are you going?"

I respond without looking back, eager to beat myself up for even thinking that I should feel bad for her, "To the nurses' station, Mother to see what **can** be done, and then outside for a smoke."

"Don't take too long Johnny."

For the second time I hear the fear in her voice and stopping at the door I hold it open as I turn back and see her, she breathes heavily, her chest moving in jagged fits and starts, her eyes wide and alert.

"I'll skip the cigarette and be right back." I manage a smile and walk out closing the door behind me.

Nineteen

———◆·❖·◆———

THREE YEARS AGO, when I was still with BDDE, and before my brief retirement and subsequent move to J. Thomas Hunt, I was given the opportunity to move to New York and work out of the main office. Just the idea that BDDE thought of bringing me up to work exclusively on national campaigns was a very big deal. I had been to New York before of course, quite a few times as a matter of fact, for meetings and corporate parties. But never for more than a couple of days at a time, and always staying mid-town near the Madison Avenue office, once or twice they even put me up at the Waldorf on Park Avenue. New York for me back then was fun and exciting and when you are on a corporate expense account, it can very well be a playground for adults. Where else can you eat raw fish for supper for a thousand bucks a person, charge it to your clients, walk outside to Columbus Circle, buy a two dollar hotdog because you're still hungry and not feel any sense of remorse? When they made me the offer of moving up, and in order to give me the chance to experience life as a New Yorker, BDDE had me come up for a month (July) to oversee the tail end of a project they had just ripped away from another creative director. They sublet a corporate apartment for me in a brand new Chelsea high rise and I got to experience the day-to-day life of living in the big city. Thirty days later, I was back in New Orleans sitting at the bar of the Columns Hotel, telling my co-workers why I had turned down the New York job, probably screwed my chance at every getting the offer ever again and yet happily returned to my home and my home town vowing never to leave her for any other city for the rest of my life. I talked about packed rush hour subways, the city smelling like a large foot, how the people there work full days on Fridays except during the summers and that for the most part, New York wasn't the New York of the movies, but the New York of endless Pottery Barns, Gaps and William Sonomas. Most importantly I told them how the days there seem to pass by in a seemingly endless stream of the "have to's" until the calendar loses all of the lines and markings that separate the days, weeks and months.

The difference for me, is that New Orleans lives on its own time, which along with the architecture of the French Quarter, and corrupt politicians are the last remaining vestiges of years of European rule. The workweek as an example, in an unwritten rule, ends on Thursday evening, with Fridays used for long lunches and early happy hours. Natives to the city spend their days with Zen-like attention to the rituals of life, food, drink, church, conversation, friends and family. People in New Orleans choose to work to live, as opposed to Manhattan, where for the most part the type A's live to work. New Yorkers for some reason are intensely proud of how much and how long they work and infuse that pride in every conversation, regardless of subject matter. To put the difference in a conversational tone, in New York the second question a person asks upon introduction is 'What do you do?'; in New Orleans, it's 'Who's your mamma?'. This is why I returned; this is why despite a horrendous diet of deep fried foods and bordelaise sauce, heart disease is no worse in New Orleans than anywhere else. And this is why, as I lay here in bed at three thirty in the morning on All Saints Day, trying to get my bearings from a moderate Halloween night of drinking, and after having just been woken up by my frantic father begging me to come help look after my mother, who seems to be suffering some sort of dementia, I can't manage to come to terms with how I have somehow let six full weeks of life slip through my fingers.

Mother has returned to the hospital, to the same floor and the same bed she had occupied before being sent to rehab and then on to a dreadful netherworld of healthcare known as skilled nursing. While in skilled nursing, mother aided her recuperation by losing her appetite and becoming increasingly depressed, even for her. I have to go to my father, so I get out of bed and see that I have inadvertently saved time by having passed out completely dressed, including my coat and shoes. I pour cold coffee from the percolator into a cup and nuke it for 90 seconds in the microwave while I spend the time looking about for my keys and wallet. Out the door, to the car and soon I'm mindlessly speeding through the early morning darkness and across the twin spans wondering for the first time what it would be like when she finally dies, and am unable to come up with any kind of scenario. I pull into the mostly empty parking lot at a little before five in the morning and rush into the hospital.

I hear mother's voice, as I get closer to her room, it sounds like she is singing. As I walk up to the closed door of her room I recognize the song, an old Glenn Miller tune called "Gal from Kalamazoo". I open the door to find my mother trying to sit up while my father is caught between laughing and trying to get her to lay back down and get quiet.

"Come on, Mother, please you have to settle down"

"How long has she been like this?" I ask approaching the bed and walking around to take my mother's other side. She is surprisingly forceful in her resistance and seems to have regained a lot of her strength. As I try to help by grabbing her shoulders, she swats at my hands and belts out the chorus, "K-A-L-A-M-A-Z-O-Oh what a gal! A real pip-er-roo...!"

Her singing the old swing tune makes me think of Sunday drives that our family used to take over to this area when we were kids. My father tricking Harry and I into the day trip by promising us ice cream, which we got only after two or three hours of driving in seemingly endless loops around north shore towns like Bentwood, Covington and Abita Springs. He liked looking at real estate for sale, in a dream of a retirement spent lounging about a rocker on a front porch that never managed to materialize. Eight track tapes of Glenn Miller, Artie Shaw, Benny Goodman and a host of other swing bands provided the soundtrack of our trips and to this day the sounds of their music reminds me of backseats, windows rolled down to let in the breeze created by the steady speed of the old Ford LTDs or Cadillac Coupes that highlighted my father's fondness for big cars.

"She started yesterday at skilled nursing, some sort of hospital psychosis they think, they have given her a sedative but it doesn't seem to help."

"Can't they give her more?"

"Not with her heart the way it is." My father leans in to her and begs mother, "Come on dear, you have to go to sleep." She quiets a little, mumbling something only she can understand, and lies back onto the pillow. "She hasn't slept since a nap yesterday morning."

"Holy shit, you gotta be kidding me. How does she have the energy for this?"

As if cued my mother looks at me, sits up and starts talking again, "I don't care what the other kids are doing, John, they are all descendants of criminals and you don't need to behave like that just to be like them." She's talking about the Melancons, the family that lived behind us for a while when I was in the fifth grade. I remember when she said that the first time, after I had watched the Krewe of Hercules parade with a couple of the older Melancon kids and got in trouble for fighting with some other older kids who weren't from our neighborhood, a middle class turf war, if you will. The Melancons were fanatical Catholics, right down to a god-awful big crucifix that hung right over their living room couch, but a bit shaky morally. The kids explained it to me that since they went to confession on every Saturday, pretty much any behavior was fair game because God forgave them. They weren't all that great to play with, but Mary Melancon, their youngest daughter and a sixth grader, introduced me to the concept of sex when she let me and two of my friends look at her naked for a buck a piece. They moved to New Orleans East before we could find out what five bucks apiece would get us.

I decided just to go along with mother's dementia, "Okay Mother, I won't."

She yawns and lies back down, "I think she might actually be getting sleepy", my dad says, yawning himself.

"Look", I say as I walk over to him, "the other bed is empty, why don't you lay down and try and get some sleep yourself?"

My father nods his head, turns and shuffles the three feet over to the other bed, I see that he is moving like a beaten old man and I also see the continuing cost that my mother's condition is having on him. I try to imagine coming to see her every day like he does and a wave of nausea passes over me. He lowers the bedrail, sits briefly on the side, swings his feet up shoes and all, and drops his head onto the pillow. I look down at mother, her eyes are open just enough so that I can see the pale whites just under her pupils. I lean in a bit to look closer and my heart skips a beat until I see that she is indeed breathing, though her breaths are so infrequent and shallow as to be almost undetectable. I walk around the end of the bed past her feet and catch myself trying to get as far from the one in the cast as possible, the image of the open wounds on the bottom still fresh in my mind. I get to the other bed as my father heaves a sigh and pulls the thin wool blanket up to cover himself to his chin.

"Don't put that too close to your mouth, god knows what kind of germs are living on that thing." *I really hate hospitals.*

"Is she asleep?"

"I think so although her eyes are still open a little."

"The medication does that."

"That's creepy."

"I know."

"You come here every day?"

"Yep, every day."

"How long do you stay?"

"I usually get here around eleven, stay until one or so, go get lunch, then come back around three and stay until they tell me to leave usually around ten or eleven at night."

"Everyday?"

"Everyday." My dad turns on his side facing the wall away from me. "Not always the same times, but pretty close."

"You can't be spending all your time here, it's not good for you." My father doesn't say anything, I look at him lying on the bed and see and hear his breathing, fifty or so years of smoking and even the deaf can hear his breathing. "It's not that bad Johnny, I've made friends with the staff, even the new ones, they watch out for me. We talk…sometimes we go out to the smoking area together."

"You smoke with the nurses?"

"…and some of the doctors."

"That's just great, when you have your heart attack, you'll be well attended. As healthcare workers, don't they know smoking is unhealthy or has that information not trickled down to LSU's medical school?"

"Why are you so sarcastic?"

"I can't help it, it was genetically inherited from her." I point back to where mother, her eyes still slightly open, is snoring in quick short bursts. "Is she alright?"

"She's fine, it's the medication."

"You can't come here every day, Dad."

"Why not?"

"Because, it's not healthy for you, you look tired…and old."

"I am tired and old."

"Yeah, but you never used to look it."

"You were too hung over on Saturdays to notice."

"Regardless Pop, you can't keep doing this."

"I have to." He turns back from the far wall to look at me.

"Why do you have to?"

"Because, there is no one else."

Oh dear god, there it is, he is waiting for me to say that I will come and help him take care of her. No, it's not to take care of her, because he doesn't really take of her when she's in the hospital, the staff does that. He wants me to help him *watch* her. But watch her what? Die? Sorry, but I don't want to be here for that. I can't look at my father so I turn and watch my mother lost in her drug induced sleep. Her breathing is short, but rhythmic…

And Mother dear, you are definitely going to die, and if I had to guess from looking at you this morning, I'd say probably sooner rather than later. Look around you Mother, your husband knows it, I certainly know it and the hospital staff knows it best of all. Because Mother, like Harry before you, are violating the first rule of the living. What is that first rule of the living you ask? The first rule of the living is that a person has to want to live, simple enough right? You don't want to live, fine, call Kevorkian…move to Oregon…do whatever. I don't give a damn, that's your choice. But I'm telling you here and now, you want to be a part of my life, you want me to care, to have sympathy for you, to help take care of you, but you still want to die then screw you. There is enough death in this world, I want people in my life who want to live so desperately that they will fight with every ounce of energy they have for one more breath, one more instant on this mortal coil. If that ain't you, then fuck off. So guess what Mother dear...

"I have to go back into the city and get some things." I tell my father before he closes his eyes.

"Things for what?" My father wants to hear me say it and I suspect somewhere underneath her sedation my mother wants to hear me say it as well.

"Things so that I can stay out here and help you with mother..." *Dammit, where is this guilt coming from? I'm a goddamn protestant,* "...I'll help with the nights."

"You're a good kid Johnny."

"No, I'm not."

Twenty

I LIFT MY head to the sound of the knocking at my office door, see a small puddle of spit where the corner of my mouth was resting on my desk, am surprised at how comfortable the top of my desk is, and how little sleep I am actually able to live with. I have been commuting daily between my parent's apartment and the office for a little over a week now. Every day I climb into my car between 6:15 and 6:30 in the morning, stopping at Tastee Donuts on Northshore Boulevard for coffee, then easing out onto Interstate ten for the ninety minute commuter wrestling match from Bentwood to downtown New Orleans. I don't understand the commuting mentality, the willingness of a person to live one, two or even three hours each way from where they work. For me personally, as my friends in Lafourche Parish say, I'd rather take a beatin' than commute to the city. The knock sounds again on my office door and I slowly get up, rub my eyes, cover the spit with paper and walk to the door. Aussie Bob is just about to walk away as I open it, "Oh hey bro, I figured you weren't there."

"What's up Bob?" I wipe the corner of my mouth with my sleeve as I speak.

"I just passed Will as I was coming out of the edit suite; he said he was lookin' for you."

"How was he?"

Bob turned and scratched his head, "'How was he how?"

"Well Bob, was he mad? Was he happy? Did he look like he wanted to kick my ass?"

"I don't know bro, I try not to get that close to 'im"."

"Thanks, you've been a big help."

I get to Will's space, down the hall from mine and see Bernadette sitting at her desk, her computer screen is turned a bit outward so that I can see that she is shopping online. "Is he in?" I interrupt her as she peruses Tiffany's site, it looks like the sterling silver collection.

"Yeah, he was looking for you"

"And, here I am."

"Lemme tell him you are here." She reaches for the phone and pushes the button that accesses the speaker; from inside the office I hear Will's extension ring. "John Hanson is out here for you." Over the speaker I hear Will moving about, "Give me a minute will ya, I'm just finishing up some copy."

"You got it."

Bernadette turns the phone off and looks up at me, "I'll just sit over here." I say motioning to the sofa sitting against the large front window of the office. Outside, on St. Charles Avenue I see a street car stop to let on passengers and notice for the first time that people outside are wearing jackets, some how with everything going on and walking around in a sleepless daze, Autumn moved in overnight, and the heavy humidity has given way to drier, cooler air that makes a person forget just how much they sweat the rest of the year.

"You look tired." Bernadette, having either finished shopping or waiting for another site to load looks over the corner of her desk at me, "I hear you're stayin' over at your momma's place while she's in the hospital."

"Yeah." I look back outside; the streetcar rumbles off, I'm not in the mood to talk.

"That's really nice of you to do that for your daddy."

"I guess so, you know, I'm just…"

"Jess says she's really sick."

"Who?"

"Your momma."

"Yeah". She gets quiet, perhaps sensing that this isn't a conversation I want to have.

"I remember when my Aunt Barbra, was sick in the hospital, last year, you were here then right?" *She's not stopping, I should've known better.*

"I don't know…"

"She had to go into St. Bernard Parish Memorial, out offa Judge Perez Drive, you know where that is?"

"I think…" I look around, and then stand.

Bernadette is looking back at her screen. "So anyway she was in that place for something like two weeks and my cousin Ant'ny, her only son, the son she sweated over, working two shifts waitin' tables at Clarence and Lefty's for; he never did so much as drop by to see how she's doin'." I start to sweat, for some reason my breath is shortening, my heart is climbing up my throat looking for a place to jump out. I get up off the sofa, Bernadette senses my anxiety, but then again I must look like a nut case, so how can she not?

"He'll be right out, I know he wants to talk to you."

"What about B...?" I stop mid sentence because I can't help but see that's she's looking at Victoria's Secret and the thought of Bernadette stuffing her rather full figure into a Vicky's Secret ensemble almost renders me motionless. I fight through the feeling and start to cross in front of her desk heading back for the hallway when Will's door opens.

"Hey," Will's smiling at me, a slick smooth grin that reminds me of the Grinch when he has his idea to hit the Whos for all their presents on Christmas Eve. "Leaving already? Man it's hard to tie you down. Come on in."

I walk into his office, a jangled mess of cardboard containers of products, cd's, clothing, old food containers, the odd Rosary or two slung about and pictures of Presidents Reagan, Bush the First and Bush the Second. Will is very proud of his conservative religious and political beliefs. The space smells oddly of lilac, until I notice that each of the four wall plugs on each of the four walls has one of those small electric air fresheners. I take a breath and can't help myself.

"It smells like a brothel in here."

"Yeah, that's Bernadette trying to tell me I need to air out and open my door every once in a while, but you know, it's hard to be creative when you get all the noise from the rabble in the halls. Sit down somewhere."

"Un-huh." I look for a place to sit but every stick of furniture is covered with some kind of crap.

"Here. Hold on." Will walks over to a chair a takes a box full of pictures and drawings that must've been done by his kid and tosses it behind a small couch that lies smothered in pizza boxes, tennis shoes and two green lawn bags, the contents of which I am truly too frightened to imagine. He pushes the chair up to the side of his desk, "Here ya go..." I sit in the chair and back it up far enough to put my foot up on the corner of the desk and recline, knowing that my informality grates on him. Will drops back into the chair behind his desk and looks at his laptop, punches a couple of keys, then looks up, "So?"

"So you were looking for me right?"

He taps and moves his finger along the touch pad that serves as the mouse. "Right...right..."

I hate this, I hate that he can't pay attention for two minutes, just as he hates it when I tire of this behavior and walk out of the office, like I've done whenever we meet. I know it's a power play; Will has had trouble with me since I got here, even though he was the one who recruited me for J. Thomas Hunt, calling me himself when I took off from BDDE

"Look, Will if you're busy…" I get up; ready to play the game with him.

"No…No…sit back down, just looking at an e-mail from the New York office." What I really want to do is call him on whatever it is he is doing. Get up, hurry around the desk and hopefully catch him cruising Hugeknockers. com or some such bullshit, instead I sit quietly.

"Okay…" he says, finally looking up and closing the top of his computer, "…here's the deal. The New York office wants us to look at a campaign they gave to one of their big shot in-house people that really screwed the pooch. We fix this and we get the account, needless to say it could be very good for all of us. I'm told them I'd give them my suggestions, but I wanted you to look at it first." Will-speak for I don't know what the fuck I'm going to do.

"You do, huh?" I say suspiciously.

I sit back looking him right in the eyes. He meets my look then opens his laptop again, waits for the screen to come up, taps the mouse pad, sighs, looks out of the window.

"Look Johnny, I know that I am not that creative, I try but it's just not in me. You are, you can visualize something, see it, and make sense with it. If we can fix this campaign it would mean finally making the big bucks, for both of us, we could present us as a team, running the show together. I can't do it alone any more, and to be honest I don't want to."

"I don't know Will, my mother's sick, and probably dying…" *Do I have the balls to use her condition again? Yes. For what, more money? Yes. I am not a good son. So what?*

"…So I got to spend time across the lake with my father. And to be straight with you, I would want more money for something like this."

"How much more?"

"I don't know, I would have to think about it and get back to you."

"Do that, by all means, just get back to me tomorrow; New York wants answer by lunch time."

"Tomorrow?"

"They want us to move on this fast. Look, I know I'm gonna say yes, you say no to something like this and you're doin' crappy local furniture ads for the rest of your life, so you gotta say yes, you know what I'm saying?"

"Alright, I'll get back to you first thing in the morning." I start to get up out of the chair.

"Hey, you hear about Jess getting back with her dude?"

'Her dude'? Since when did we teleport back to 1977?

"Yeah, I heard something about that?"

"She's kind of flaky right? I mean she comes from all that money and still works. What's that about? Still, she's kind of hot in a weird sort of way." Will grins from behind his computer. I turn and hurry to the door before I reach back and hit him with every ounce of strength I can muster. You want to take my work and use it for your own? Fine, I don't care. But you start talking about the woman I still love? Watch the fuck out, 'dude'! Though I do hate that I still love her…

"Yeah…no…I don't…" I am stammering as I open the door, Will stands behind me, he has become the Grinch again.

"Bernadette, can you come in here?"

Bernadette titters, so help me God she titters, then slides her chair back, smoothes her skirt and slides past me into the office. The door closes, and as I walk down the hall I hear the latch throw locking them in.

The meeting has sent me spinning into a funk. The last thing I want right now is a good reason not to pick up what few things I want from my office and walk out of the door. But, dammit, this is a good reason. I have been in this business for a long time and for a long time I have managed without making really nice money and by 'really nice money' I mean enough money so that I don't have to think twice about buying clothes, or a new television or whatever. Don't get me wrong, I do okay, but I never manage to ask for what I feel I am entitled to, this is a virus that has plagued every aspect of my life since I was a kid, and in the end it is always me who has suffered for it. Besides, money equals respect right, and we can all use more respect. So tomorrow, screw it, I'll ask for the moon and let Will counter, I'll counter back and we'll negotiate and negotiation is good for the soul. But, if I do decide to stay it means having to work alongside of Jess for another year at least. I have managed to stay away from her for the last few weeks for the most part, since she and I have been working on separate projects. It also helps that every time I see her I demonize her by turning her into a mythological emasculating witch, mostly by putting words into her mouth that she never said and by constantly visualizing her sitting down to a healthy lunch of my heart and soul. Childish, I know but hey, any port in a storm right? So it's settled. I know that Will needs me, he pretty much confessed that to me just now, so he will have to give in on something, mostly the money, and in spite of having to see and work with Jess, I'll just grit my teeth, bear it and beat the living shit out of anyone that tells me any part of what is or isn't going on in her life. I leave the office feeling pretty good about myself, in spite of the fact that I have an hour and a half drive and another hour or two at hospital looming ahead of me.

I get into the office at eight-thirty the next day and pace back and forth in my office until Will shows up at nine-thirty. I am in his office by ten and by ten thirty he has looked at my offer and told me in effect that he can't afford me and I would have to take the project at my current salary. By eleven o'clock on the morning of November tenth, I have packed my things and walked out of the door. By eleven thirty I am on my second drink.

Twenty-One

———◆·❈·◆———

"So, WHAT ARE you going to do for money?"

"I don't know."

I am sitting on a cast iron bench located on the third floor terrace of the hospital that my father has made into his own personal smoker's lounge, just down the hall from my mother's room.

"It's not like there are a hundred agencies in New Orleans, you pretty much burned your bridges with the only two that are worth a damn."

"I know."

"So I ask you again, what are going to do for money?"

"And I say again, I don't know. I'm not going to worry about it." My father tosses his cigarette down to the concrete floor of the terrace and snuffs it out with his foot. A fresh crew cut has his hair standing up Fuller Brush thick and straight. I notice that he is dressed in his usual out fit of "putter" pants and short sleeve knit with pocket for cigarettes, but now his added a Mr. Rogers zip up blue cardigan and is also wearing orthopedic tennis shoes with Velcro closures instead of laces. I think back to when he used to wear maroon penny loafers almost all of the time, the exception being the black or brown wingtips that he wore to work and church. When I was a kid I used to clop around in his loafers and he would tease me by telling me that I wouldn't be a man until I filled his shoes. When I was fifteen I finally slipped my foot in with the help of a shoehorn and went to him and asked him if I was a man because I could fit into his shoes. He made a fist and hit me square in the jaw,

136

knocking me to the floor. As I shook off the cobwebs, he laughed and leaned over me, "Not yet," was all he said.

"Hey!" my father has raised his voice snapping me out of my alcohol induced fugue state, "What are you thinking about? Have you been drinking?"

"I had a couple after I left work."

"I thought you were laying off for a while, I thought we both were."

"Yeah, well I had some extenuating circumstances, wouldn't you say?"

"So you aren't going to look for anything?"

"Not right now, no."

"How are you going to pay your bills?"

"I got enough to last me for a couple of months, maybe four if I stretch."

My father sat quietly looking out towards the parking lot, reached into his jacket and took out his cigarettes and lit another.

"What about us?" he says taking a drag.

"Us who?"

"Your mother and I? What happens to us if you don't work? Our lives suffer too, or haven't you thought about that?"

"So, let me get this straight, when Will blew me off today, when he blew off the fact that I had carried him and his agency for the whole year, by telling me I wasn't worth the very reasonable price I was asking. I was supposed to think of you two before getting pissed and walking out?"

"You should of thought of the ramifications of your actions on other people John, and not just have been thinking of yourself. Your mother and I need the money you give us."

"And you wonder why I drink." I say as I get up. The door that leads back inside opens and one of the third floor nurses sticks her head out, "Dr. Harris is here and he wants to talk to ya'll." I feel the butterflies build in my stomach as I turn back to see my father's face go an ashen gray. He flicks his cigarette over the railing of the terrace and together we walk back into the hospital.

We enter the hospital and follow the hallway around to Three West where we see Doctor. Harris standing at the nurse's station thumbing through a patient's binder. We have to pass mother's room to get to the station and as we do I pause, the television is on, tuned to the New Orleans CBS affiliate. The five o'clock news with Bill Elder is on, it's the only news broadcast she'll watch. Doctor Harris hands the binder back to the black nurse's aide seated at the station's desk and turns to meet us. "Ya'll want coffee, 'cause I sure could use a cup; I got a bit of the afternoon doldrums."

"I could use a cup, you Dad?"

"Sure."

"Great," says Harris turning back to the desk, "Claudet, tell Adrienne I'll be back to check on Mr. Robicheaux in twenty minutes."

"Sure thang, Docta Harris." Claudette responds as she stamps a page in the binder.

"Let's go then, I'll buy." Harris smiles as he takes my father's elbow; I notice that he seems a bit too cheerful as I follow them to the stairwell.

"Well, she is definitely slipping. Her levels are inconsistent, her blood sugar ranges from twenty to six hundred, her heart is working on somewhere around thirty percent and we have to medicate her to keep her kidneys working." We have just taken our seats in the cafeteria as Doctor Harris gives us the news. My eyes are having a hell of a time focusing and my head was beginning to hurt from not having a drink in a couple of hours. My father sits absent-mindedly staring into and stirring his coffee.

"Doc, she's been slipping for months, years, I don't see how this is new to any of us."

Doctor Harris takes a sip of his coffee, some of it drools down the front of his white coat, "Damn I can't keep anything white for any length of time, I swear, " as he uses his white lab coat sleeve to rub at the stain, "This is new John because your mother has a DNR and I want to know what to do if she codes."

I look at my father, "What do you mean 'what to do'? She has a "Do Not Resuscitate" order, I'm guessing you would…"

"Keep her alive", my father interrupts, but he doesn't look at either Doctor Harris or me as he says this.

"What?" I am truly surprised at my father, it seems that if any one wanted to let her go, if any one had been through a real shit hole of a life for the last five years it would've been him.

"Keep her alive Doc, I'm not ready to lose her."

"Yeah but…"

"You don't know Johnny, it's been almost sixty years for the two of us, I don't remember what it's like to be alone and I'm not ready for it, I'm not ready to face that." We sit quietly, the three of us; I think my father has even caught Doctor Harris off guard.

"I have to get back upstairs, this isn't something we have to determine right this very instant, though it's better to discuss it now and be prepared." Doctor Harris puts a hand on my father's shoulder, "She doesn't want to stay, Sean and she hasn't for a while, remember that."

"So what you're saying is we do an assisted suicide."

"No, Sean, I'm saying we…you need to let her go."

Dr. Harris releases my father and walks toward the doors of the cafeteria, my father stirs his coffee and looks off into the distance; he focuses on some point off into the distance, his eyes soft and glassy.

"You never prepare for this Johnny, no one ever prepares you for this."

"For what dad?"

"For the ending, we are prepared for everything else in life but we are never prepared for the ending." My dad lifts the cup of coffee to his mouth and takes a sip. My own coffee looks to be as incredibly hot as his is from the steam rising above the rim of the Styrofoam cups, but he doesn't seem to notice. "Your mother and I have known each other for seventy years. We got married because I was leaving for a stint in the service...were we in love? I don't know...we were kids, what did we know about love? But we sure thought we did, so the weekend before I left we ran to the justice of the peace and we got married. When I got out of the service and came back...Shit Johnny, we hadn't spent two days together before I left for two years and the next thing you know here we are, two married strangers living in her parent's house. The time apart because of the war had changed us, somewhere in all of that and while we were apart, we had grown up. I didn't know her from Adam's cat and she sure didn't know me, but we decided to try. She was working as a secretary and I got a job at a lumberyard. After we paid our bills we didn't have a dime between us so we stayed in on weekends and got to know each other by talkin'. It took four months of living together, she in the bedroom and me on the couch before your mother would have sex with me but we did."

"I really don't think that..." My father ignores me and I become terrified that he is going to give me more details of their sex life.

"It was okay, you know, the whole being poor thing, because we knew we would work through it. In the beginning the whole reason we spent so much time at your grandparents' house was because there were a lot of times we just didn't have the money for food. But we stuck it out and gradually things changed. We prepared for everything, for moving when the job said we had to, for not having kids when we thought we would and then having them when we thought we wouldn't. You and your brother were both surprises you know, but since we had prepared before, well we knew what to do. Even though we were older by then. When your mother got sick I was there, when I was sick she was there..."

I am finished with my coffee and not wanting to look up I stare into the empty cup. This is the most my father has ever said to me in one sitting and now seems to be on the verge of crying and I just don't think that I am up for that right now so I stand up, "I know you guys were there for each other but, now I think we ought to..."

"Shut the fuck up Johnny and sit back down!" My father looks at me and the anger in his eyes stuns me more than his use of the word 'fuck', a word

I have never heard him say, not even on the golf course. I ease myself back into the chair, looking side to side to see if anyone else heard him and may be thinking that perhaps I brought my crazy grandfather down for coffee. My father leans across the table and grabs me by the arm and pulls me close to him, his voice is urgent his eyebrows forming a harsh "V".

"You need to listen to this because one day it will be you." My father lets go of me and slides back in his chair with a sigh, "One day Johnny you will open your eyes and you will realize that your life has past and if you are not careful and if you do not pay attention and if you lose yourself as it is so easy to do in the things that are transitory and meaningless, then you will find that your life has passed and you will have nothing to show for it, not even love. You will find yourself talking with your own son about spending your entire adult life with someone you knew and loved, but who never really loved you. How you had thousands of moments where you looked at each other and knew that she didn't love you, but knew you couldn't have gotten where you were without her. You will tell him about how in spite of that, in spite of the not loving, you still prepared for everything that life had to dish out because that is what two people are supposed to do. How you planned and mapped, bought the things you needed and wanted, houses, cars, vacations, and schools, how you lived the typical American Baby Boomer life. But that life never prepared you for when that other person wouldn't be there any more. There were a hundred times over the course of our marriage when I wanted to say goodbye, Johnny, a hundred times I wanted to walk out of the door, but I couldn't bear the thought of being alone That's why I never left, not because of her or Harry or you, but because I was just too scared." My father sits slumped in his chair; I have no idea what to say to him, what do you say to that? I suppose I knew deep down that Mother didn't really love him, but I never would have thought that he was even remotely aware. My father sips his coffee, takes a breath and stands up.

"I guess in some ways that is love, I guess in most ways it's not. Regardless, I still can't say goodbye, I'm still not ready to be alone Johnny and I am still scared. I'm going to go back up to your mother, you coming?"

"In a minute."

"Maybe I'll go have a cigarette out front first." He says taking the pack out of his jacket pocket.

"Pop…"

"Yeah, Johnny?"

"I'm sorry."

"Don't be sorry for me Johnny and don't be sorry for your mother either. We had a good partnership, we made good decisions together, we had a good life except for the last few years, but I don't have any regrets."

His composure regained, his demeanor having returned to that of the man I have known my whole life, my father turns and walks out of the cafeteria to go sit at the bedside of a dying woman he had known and lived with for most of his life, but, by his own admission, never loved him. I sit and wonder how it is that two people can meet as children, grow up together, marry, have children of their own, spend time together, go to the country club dances, buy houses, sell houses, drive big cars, have checking accounts, savings accounts, Christmas accounts and every credit card for every department store and bank there is, be with each other through sickness and health, in essence, do all of the things two people have to do to achieve the American Dream and not once in all that time ever truly love each other. I am beginning to think that if love is not innate, if the ability to love another is not a part of who we are inherently, if the act of loving, truly deeply loving another person is something that we must model and learn from those around us, then I am fucked. Then as if I were Paul of Tarsus on the road to Damascus to help my fellow Jews stone the early Christians, a great light blinds me. Maybe in a certain sense Mother is right about Harry, maybe he did die because of love, but not that he didn't get any from those around him, but that he didn't know what to do with the love he got and he certainly didn't know how to love back. Maybe that's why he hated himself so much.

I look around the crowded cafeteria to see the tables jammed with staff, visitors and patients all adding to a cacophony of noise so great that it is hard to imagine this a place for dying. I look around and immediately feel very alone…and very afraid.

Twenty-Two

My NEW CELL phone is ringing. I know this in spite of the fact that I am somewhere far away from it. I am in a dark place, and I am upset, but my phone is ringing and I don't know why I am upset so I sit up, turn on the bedside light and reach for my phone. The caller I.D says it is a private caller; I hesitate thinking it is bad news but as the fog clears I realize that if my mother were dead my father would probably just walk across the short hallway of their apartment, open the door and tell me himself. I throw caution to the breeze and answer it, "Hello?"

"How are you doing?"

Dear god, it's Jess, I pick up my watch from the nightstand. "Fine I guess. You do know its two thirty in the morning."

"I am entirely aware of the time." She laughs, she's been drinking,

"You've been drinking,"

"Wrong," she says firmly, "I am currently drinking." For some reason I am getting pissed off at her.

"Where's your husband?"

"He's not my husband, asshole," I hear her take a sip, "Any way, he's at some buddy's camp preparing to go slaughter huge numbers of waterfowl, my daughter went to my parents and I went out with some friends, got home and wanted to see how you were doing because I was thinking about you."

"You were thinking about me?"

"Yesh."

"Thank you Jess, I appreciate that you were thinking about me, but I think you should probably go to bed now."

"I don't want to."

The last thing I want to do is argue with a moderately drunk, head strong woman who I am still in love with but who also currently lives with her ex-non-ex husband. "Then do what you want to Jess, I'm tired, I've been splitting time with my father at the hospital."

"Too tired to come and see me?"

"What?"

"I said are you too tired to come and see me?"

"Jess, as I said it's two thirty…nope, now it's two thirty-five in the morning and you have to go to work tomorrow…today."

"I know what time it is and I don't have to go to work today and I want to see you, I want to talk to you, I miss talking to you."

"And you had to get drunk to tell me that?"

"Look, you're killing my buzz, buddy, do you want to come see me or what?"

"Jess, I would crawl naked over broken glass to see you."

"You might want to drive, if you crawl it'll take days."

"I'll be there in an hour."

"I'll put coffee on, I could use some."

"That's good, but I could use a drink."

"I have that too, I'll see you in an hour", with that she hangs up. I hop out of bed and dress, my heart racing, both from fear and excitement, the perfect fight or flight scenario. "Damn her…" I say out loud to the photos of my dead brother as I struggle to get my jeans on. I get dressed, grab my keys and wallet and walk out of the spare bedroom to find my father sitting at the kitchen table wearing only his boxers and smoking a cigarette.

"What are you doing up?" He picks his cigarette up from the ancient ashtray that he keeps on the kitchen counter. I think of him and mother flicking their ashes in it while sitting at the table when I was a kid.

"I heard your phone ring, thought it might be the hospital, that maybe something was wrong with the house phone, so I got up to check it and figured I have a smoke. You mother's not here so I don't have to smoke outside. You going somewhere?"

"Yeah, I got to run into the city and see a friend, someone I used to work with."

"At this time of the night?"

"Yeah, I'll still be back to go to the hospital at noon to relieve you, go on back to bed."

"What kind of friend wants you to come over in the middle of the night?"

"Good night dad." I throw a jacket on, grab my keys and hurry out of the door. I laugh at myself as I walk down the stairs, finding it humorous that at forty years old I still can't tell my father what I am doing and still maintain that childhood fear of reprimand.

I manage to cover that same ground that takes over ninety minutes in morning and evening rush hour in roughly half that amount of time at three o'clock in the morning. As I exit off of I-610 onto the Ponchartrain Expressway doing a cool ninety I am convinced my car is going to blow apart at the seams, but she is holding together. I call Jess from the car, to make sure she is still awake and in fact still wants me to come over, the phone rings three times and I admit that there is a part of me that for some reason doesn't want her to answer but she finally picks it up.

"Hey, I'm close but I just wanted to call and see if you still wanted me to come by."

"You're a Jackass."

"Is that a yes?"

Jess is sitting on her porch drinking a cup of coffee as I pull up in front of her house. I haven't been back to her house since we'd stopped seeing each other and haven't even seen her since my last morning at work over three weeks ago. My heart is beating so fast I'm sure she can hear it. I park behind her car in the driveway and step from the door as she opens the screen and comes down off of the porch to meet me. As I watch her move an emptiness expands within me, it is as if everything inside of me is gone, everything except for my heart which is left hanging precariously like a hero in an old action film clutching to edge of the cliff by his fingernails, would he fall, or would he be rescued at the last minute? She walks up and without saying anything wraps her arms around me, startling me, but I quickly gain my head and hug her back just as tightly. "And hello to you darlin'" I choke on the words.

"You are always so huggable"

"Is that a nice way to say fat?"

"You are not fat," she says laughing, "Come on up, you want coffee or a beer?"

"Coffee and chicory or American Coffee?"

"I got it from the French Market when I went shopping for a shoot, its fresh ground with chicory."

"Then I'll have both, beer and coffee."

"The poor man's speed ball." She laughs as she darts through the front door, "Come on in." She calls back over her shoulder. I enter Jess' house slowly looking for the signs of male occupation, not knowing what exactly that would be given what I know of her ex, jock straps and Penthouse magazines? Used bullet casings with the odd deer head lying about? Cro-Magnon drawings of primitive spear toting hunter-gatherers pursuing mammoths on the living room walls?

No such luck, her shotgun, laid out much in the same manner of my rental house, looks the same as it did the last time I saw it; up-scale department store furniture surrounded by Jess' art, collected from friends which includes everything from an impressionist oil of Long Vue Gardens, (a beautiful classic revival house with an English style garden that sits on the border between New Orleans and Metarie) that was done by one of the more accomplished French Quarter artist to a large canvas of a woman reminiscent of Picasso in his blue period, with large almond shaped eyes, striking features and painted by an eccentric, color blind psychiatrist who once lived around the corner from her on Bienville Street.

"She's my favorite." Jess returns, pointing to the woman with the hand carrying coffee.

"I know, still I can't help thinking that if the guy is a psychiatrist, then is everything he paints a Rorschach?"

"I don't know, I'll ask him when I see him again. Take your coat off, stay a while."

"Are you sure, I mean I got to say it feels a little odd being here."

"Why? What's odd about it?"

"Come on, Jess, stop it. You know what's odd about this."

She puts the drinks down on the coffee table and walks behind me and takes my jacket off, "You mean calling you at two-thirty in the morning?" She sits on the sofa.

"No…well yes, but for you it's really not that odd, it's more about the fact that you are living with your ex-husband." I sit next to her and take a big sip of the beer. "Oh, that."

"Yes, that."

I look at her; she smiles at me, a wicked mischievous smile.

"I forgot my coffee outside", she jumps up and walks out the front door and back in, bumping her arm on the door frame and spilling some of the coffee on the hardwood floor, which she smears about with her shoe, her idea of cleaning it up. She places her coffee on the table and plops down on he sofa and turns to me, "So…?"

I am torn between love and annoyance. "So how's your husband?"

"Ex-husband"

"Is this why you asked me to come over because we really could have had this conversation on the phone."

"No, this is not why I asked you over. I have something to say to you." I drink the last of the beer down in a second gulp.

"Okay, so say it."

"Do you want another beer first?"

"Yeah, okay." Jess hops off of the sofa again and goes to the kitchen. She returns with the beer, two shot glasses and a bottle of Barbancourt that I had given her after our trip to Tim and Andy's for the Fourth.

"How about a beer and a shot and you forget about the coffee?" She sits and pours two shots for us, we drink them, wince at each other because those first shots of the Haitian rum are hell, "So what do you have to say to me?"

"I love you."

"You what?" I am so unnerved I can't look at her so I focus on the woman on the wall,

"You heard me."

I smile and turn to her, "Yes, I did, but I'm not sure I heard you correctly."

"I said that I love you."

I have no clue as to what to say or do at this moment. None. Mostly because I can't quite figure out exactly what the feelings are that seem to be tearing around in side of me at light speed, great leaping streams of joy, bewilderment, and sheer terror running through me in a great electric surge from head to hand to foot to head again.

"Okay..." is all I can manage.

"Okay what?"

Breathe Johnny, the chant begins inside my forehead, just breathe and you'll be fine, "Okay as in I have only a hundred or so questions about this." I reach over her and pour myself another shot and chase it with a long sip of beer, the Barbancourt burns just long enough for the beer to douse the flames. I take in a lot of air and let it out slowly.

"So, what kind of questions do you have?"

"Why now?" I blurt out. What I really want to ask is why now and not three months ago? But I am hyperventilating so I let the question hang and fill our shot glasses.

"Well..." she begins, then pauses to drink her shot "...Lord have mercy...I guess it's because I have had chance to think about us, to think about how it was, what it was like having someone care about me the way you did."

"Do."

"Do, right, and you care about me for reasons that still escape me."

Now it's my turn as I take my third shot of Barbancourt, the rum's burn has lessened, instead the liquor jolts briefly then eases it's way down the throat and covers the insides like an old family quilt. All tension, anxiety and excitement is giving way to a feeling of warm contentment.

"What about Stephen? Doesn't he care for you the way that I do, I mean Jesus Christ, Jess he must do something, you let him back into your life."

"Yes…I mean no, he doesn't care for me the way that you do, and I don't think any man I've ever been with has done that. And when you would say that you wanted me to be me, I believed that."

"I meant it."

"I know. Look Stephen is number one in his life and I know that he will always be number one to himself, that's just the way he is. But for me, and while I'm with him, all I want to know is that I am at least number two."

I pour another shot of rum for each of us and suddenly feel the need to walk. I'm no good at thinking while I'm sitting down, anytime I get a problem, a real problem, I feel like I'm working harder to solve it when I pace. It drove my ex-wife crazy, perhaps that's why I kept doing it. I get up and walk to the front door, close my right eye and using only my left, look out of the red pane of the stained glass window that hangs from a transom just above the traditional four paned window set within the door. Everything that sits within the range of the porch light is bathed in red. I think, *Rose colored glasses my ass* and drink my shot. I turn back to her.

"I don't get it Jess, I don't understand how you can willfully let yourself be okay with not being the most important thing in Stephen's life." I start to walk the line of the inside of the house in a counter clockwise motion,

"He knows how I feel Johnny, I've told him, and I need to see if he can do this."

"You can't change him Jess, I think that I am finally beginning to understand that regardless of best intentions one person cannot change another. And have it last anyway."

"I'm not trying to change him Johnny, I am trying to see if he will change himself and why are we talking about Steven and me anyway, this isn't why I called you." My trek to circumnavigate the living room has gotten me to my first corner, I watch her out of my left eye as I now work my way to the back of the room.

"I am lost, Jess, I don't understand why you called me, I don't understand why you're deciding now, while you're trying to work it out with Stephen, mind you, that you love me, I don't understand what I am supposed to do with this, except…never mind." I stop and look at the smeared colors of the azaleas in the painting of Long Vue, held back by the gilded frame, frozen by their capture in oil, thinner and brush stroke, never to grow, never to die, always the same.

"Except what? Never mind, what? Turn around and look at me will you?"

"Taking the risk at sounding dramatic…I was going to say except to let myself be tortured by knowing this."

"Excuse the fuck out of me!" She grabs the bottle of rum and her shot glass, pours herself a shot and drinks it down immediately, wiping her lips with the back if her hand. Then she stands and walks to the corner on the opposite side of the room, we are at one hundred and eighty degrees. "I didn't mean to drag your ass over here to torture you as you put it. I thought after all that was said and done you would want to know how you made me feel, how you exposed me, made me see me for myself." She has started to cry, not a good thing for Jess, she has always seen crying as a weakness.

"Damn it, I'm getting all girly."

I walk across the room and gingerly take her in my arms, she folds into me and to my surprise she allows the closeness. The sense of her, not just that she is a woman, but that she is *the* woman, her warmth is *the* warmth, her smell is *the* smell, and the instantaneous familiarity of being with her brings me into her and I am crushed because I have known since day one that for me there will be no other, not like her. We hold each other and stay quiet for a long time

"Look," I say separating from her slightly, "I suppose that if I am going to be tortured for the rest of my life, I can't think of anyone else I'd rather have torturing me."

She laughs, and then buries her head into my shoulder, "But I don't want to hurt you, and I don't want to torture you."

I take her and guide her back to the sofa; we sit close, her hip, side and shoulder leaning on mine. "Love is so fucked up."

She smiles, "I know, who would've thought that something so simple could be so complex."

"Maybe it is complex, maybe it isn't I don't know, I think that is what I'm really beginning to understand, that I don't know what love is." Jess turns to me, I look into her eyes and my first thought is not to get drawn in, because in the last five minutes it has become clear exactly what is and what is not to be between us.

"If you don't know what love is, then how do you know that you love me?"

"Because, though I don't know what love is, I do know what it is not. It's not what I felt before with my ex-wife, it's not what I felt for my college girlfriends, or high school girlfriends, it's not what I feel for my parents and certainly not my brother. That wasn't love, not real love anyway. The love I felt for those people was more like the kind of love that means I don't want anything bad or harmful to happen to them. That's the kind of love that has conditions, terms, clauses and most of all fear. I love you as long as…fill in the blank. Real love isn't like that, real love has none of those, it has acceptance and understanding and it doesn't have any fear."

"Johnny, everyone is afraid. You seem to think that love is what you find in story books or old movies where two people meet each other, struggle with the world around them but never struggle with themselves and at the end of all of their turmoil, they emerge from all the crap clean and neat and living happily ever after. But love isn't like that, people aren't like that, people are messy and cruel to each other and themselves. And people are afraid."

"I understand that Jess, believe me I am not naïve. I understand that people, the world and love itself is messy, but in the end, what is there to really be afraid of?" Jess sits bolt up right, not so much to get away but to make a point,

"Everything Johnny, you name it and people are afraid of it; losing their jobs, their homes, their money, death, taxes, monsters in the closet, I don't know. Pick something out and you'll find a person scared to death of it. The news is full of crap that makes us afraid, it's how they make their money. It's how we make **our** money!"

"What are you afraid of Jess?"

"Being hurt." She answers quickly, directly; I know that this is the truth.

"But you're getting back into a relationship with someone who's hurt you before and may or may not hurt you again."

"I know."

"Why?"

"Because I know him, and I believe that there is something there, something inside of him that will show itself. You know everybody talks to me about him; everybody beats me up about him. I have to have some hope. I have to believe this about him, I don't know why."

"But, still you're afraid."

"Yes." She drops her eyes from mine, it's getting close to dawn, the rum is wearing thin, I am getting tired and my head is beginning to throb at the base of my neck. I am beginning to slip into the depression that alcohol brings, depression that is only offset by continuing to drink, but I don't want to do that right now. Not here and not with Jess. I take her in my arms again, "When you say you love me, are you in love with me?"

"Yes, Johnny, I am in love with you."

"Leave Stephen and marry me." I feel the sob as it creeps out of her, like a prisoner trying to escape.

"I can't."

"But if you are in love with me…" Jess stands quickly,

"I love you Johnny more than you know and probably more than I would ever admit to myself or anyone else, but I can't be with you because I am afraid that you will disappoint me too."

"Have I yet?"

"No, you haven't."

"Then why…"

"I know it sounds fucked up, but this is the way it is and the way it has to be for now. Stephen has disappointed me before, just like you said and I guess if he does it again, well, then it's nothing new to me because I've been down that road. But you haven't, you've been wonderful to me. You have given me everything you have to give, everything you say that love is and you aren't afraid to do it."

"This is great, let me know when you get to the downside."

"The thing is Johnny, if I end it here, if it goes no farther than this, then your record is perfect. All love and no disappointment and regardless of what happens in my life I can always say that once, for a short time, I had someone love me…I…I guess that's what I've wanted to tell you all along and why I wanted you to come by tonight, to say that I know that you loved me…"

"I do love you, still."

"…And I loved you, and do love you, then and now."

"Is this it then, is this how it is going to be forever?"

"I don't like to say forever Johnny, I don't like to close doors, or if I close the doors, I want to keep the windows open."

I stand up with her, and look down into her eyes, "That's just great for you Jess, but what the hell am I supposed to do? Wait? See what comes of you and Stephen in a week, a month, a year while you keep your windows open?"

"I don't expect you to wait…are you mad at me?"

I wait, wanting more than anything for some sense of anger to rise up and take hold, so that I can swim in it for a while. But try as I might, it just won't come

"No…I'm not mad, as much as I would really like to be mad, I'm not."

I walk away from her and go to where my jacket lies tossed across an ancient flower patterned winged back chair in the corner. I look out of the window and notice a faint purple glow starting to ease through the low branches of the oaks that line Webster Street. I heave a sigh and find myself not wanting to leave, not wanting to start a new day in what I am believing will be for a while yet and terribly sad new world. I pick up my jacket and start to put it on.

"Are you going?"

"Yeah, I think it's probably a good time to leave. All of a sudden I am very, very tired."

"Tonight didn't come out quite the way I thought it would." Jess has walked up behind me, wrapped her arms around me and laid her head against my back. I don't even know if I can look at her any more, inside my heart has gone, broken from it's moorings it has drifted free with a dreadful current taking to places unknown and unexplored.

"What did you think would happen?"

"I don't know, I guess I had these hopes that my telling you I love you would make you happy, that we would laugh and talk and just share space and time the way we used to."

I turn around to her, "And what? At the end I would just walk off, happy in the knowledge that this woman that has captured every inch of my being from the day I met her has finally decided that she loves me?"

"You make it sound so harsh."

"It is harsh, Jess. I don't live in a vacuum, I know that now, and maybe, just maybe I'll meet someone and feel for them the way I feel about you, I don't know, I tend to believe that the way I feel for you happens only once in each lifetime. But up until this happens again, or if it doesn't then for the rest of my fucking life I'm going to ask myself why the fuck it didn't happen while were together so that we could have had a chance. I hate Stephen, I don't know him and I still hate him, because he gets your love blindly and he doesn't care, he just pisses all over it."

Out of habit I look down at my watch, but inside I know that it's either very late or very early depending on your outlook. "I gotta go, I have to get to the hospital by noon so my dad doesn't go off of the fucking deep end." I pull away from her and walk to the door. Jess stands still, her feet planted she looks at me, tears in her eyes. "I love you Jess, I just wish it were enough." I walk out of her front door to the sounds of the birds, and the glorious sunrise of a crisp, beautiful fall New Orleans morning. I leave her farther behind me with every step and as I walk I am becoming increasingly consumed by sadness and a filling hate for God, life and especially love.

Twenty-Three

----•◦◊◦•----

I WONDER WHAT it is like to know the hour of your death. I suppose the only people who truly know what the exact day and time of their death is are the inmates on death row; the ones who have exhausted all appeals and have nothing save the rare intervention of a governor to save them. These people know the very minute at which death will enter their body and come to claim them. I suppose that someone fully committed to taking their own life may know the exact time at which they will kill themselves, but that can vary based on their convictions and the strength of the self destruction that propels them to that end. Through my decision to help my father attend to my mother over these last few weeks I am beginning to believe that my mother may in spite of the haze of medications she is now receiving though the hole in her wrist, know the exact time of her death, but she has for the most part stopped talking.

She lies in room 317 on floor Three West of the Northshore Regional Medical Center somewhere between valid and invalid, or non-valid if you prefer. I sit at mother's bedside watching her. Less out of concern, than looking for whatever the sign will be that this is it, a last breath, a cry out to God, recognition of a long dead relative or maybe even the proverbial light at the end of the tunnel. She is wasting away in front of our eyes now, and is rarely awake, though when she is, she manages whatever strength is left to bark out some order or another. I smile at the thought that she has decided to stay bitter and angry to the very end, how attractive. My father has taken my attendance here at the hospital these past couple of weeks to represent his version of a get out of jail free card, taking off when I arrive, usually around twelve or twelve thirty in the afternoon, and not returning until five or so. Though he does use his time well; home for lunch, a nap and then off to knock back a couple of toddies with the senior crowd at one of the local watering holes. I read once where seniors are the fastest growing segment of alcoholics in the country, mainly because they have nothing better to do, or so they think. I figure why the fuck not? What is there left to remain sober for at that point in your life? Shit, I would do that now if I could.

Most of the time I try to lose myself in the television, becoming like the patients themselves, prisoners of immobility forced to endure great stretches of time with no other voice present except those on TV. With mother snoring next to me, I watch 'As The World Turns' to look at the women. I watch Oprah to find out what women are thinking and the evening news in order to see just how depressed I can become. The rest of the time I am left to think. This is the bad time. Surrounded by the noises of the hospital, the beeps and dings of the electric pumps and monitors that keep mother alive, as well as the moans and cries of the sick, I plot ways to sneak in to the locked cabinet behind the nurses station where they keep the good drugs, not the over priced garbage spewed forth from the mills of the poor struggling billion dollar conglomerates in New Jersey that may or may not help you. That is, if the side effects, conveniently not noticed in the initial FDA trial don't kill you first. I want the good drugs, the nice drugs, the ones that make feel like you could care less whether you live or die as long as you go out feeling llliiiiikeee thhhhiiiisssss. I want these drugs because when I think, I get depressed and I am depressed so often nowadays that I have trouble recalling not being depressed. Yesterday when I found myself thinking about Jess, I really wanted to get high, instead I deleted her numbers from my caller list on my cell phone. Not quite the same but in some strange way it helped.

Today, as I look at mother, her chest heaving, her eyes darting back and forth under partially open lids I find myself thinking about when Harry and I were just kids; replaying long past events, holidays, and incidents like newsreel footage, but without commentary. The images parading by and bearing silent witness that they actually occurred, though they seem in truth to not be a part of my life at all, like the infamous and manipulated footage of Hitler dancing his jig after the fall of Paris. Black, white and read all over as the kid's joke goes, I stretch back for the very first memories I have of my mother. I edit the scenes together as if I were assembling one of my commercials, remembering the moments of Mother as mother, selling her to myself in the same way I would sell coffee to the masses, images of fire places, warm blankets and the family gathered about hugging each other and laughing. I think of moments like the first day of second grade when I cried desperately about having to go to my new school. And mother finally getting me into the car, driving down St. Roch and stopping in front of, what seemed to a wildly hysterical seven year old, as the ten mile long ramp that lead up to the front doors of a school that looked like the medieval entrance of Alcatraz as pictured in the "A" volume of my beloved World Book Encyclopedia. Deciding I needed more time, Mother then drove me around the block until I was able to get my courage up enough to go into the school.

I think of walking home from school on perfect fall days, up the driveway and through the back door to the smell of cookies in the oven and cold milk and calling out the questions to Art Fleming's answers on Jeopardy or Friday night movies with stars like Bette Davis, Claudette Colbert or Cary Grant. Time shared and enjoyed between she and I because her beloved Harry as he grew into the age of junior high and high school seemed to avoid us and the house as if it had been marked with the large yellow "Y" that was painted on the houses of nineteenth century New Orleans during the outbreaks of Yellow Fever.

Then slowly the memories of mother turn from love and caring, to memories of pain caused by pointed anger often disguised as wit acerbic and dangerous. Like the time she humiliated me after she spied the love of my fifth grade life Christy Mills and her mother and then called out to them as she dragged me behind her trying to pull up my oversized Easter pants through the Husky Boys department of my father's store in order to have a useless conversation with a women she had made quite clear on several occasions she couldn't stand. After five embarrassing minutes of her describing how hard it was to find anything to fit me because I "had my father's belly" Mother sent Christy and her mom away and turned back to me and said that things like this wouldn't happen if I weren't so fat. I think of her coddling Harry after he had flunked out of his first college. How she and my dad paid Harry's tuition when he transferred to the University of New Orleans bought his books and let him live at home rent-free. When I had given up my baseball scholarship because I had hurt my arm and was unable to play any more, I was told that I was on my own as far as they were concerned. When Harry's addiction (the existence of which was denied repeatedly by my parents) was such that he couldn't take care of himself anymore and he ended up in the hospital and near death because he was too high to know he had contracted pneumonia, my father called to tell me I should come and see him because he may not make it, my response was that Harry was on his own. From then on and until Harry died, I left all three of them alone.

I look at her lying in front of me; old, dry, withered, and I imagine Harry, teeth bared to show the elongated canines of the creatures of the night as he bends over her gaining strength while drawing out whatever life force she had left. Her hands grasping him in the death lover's embrace. I realize now that I loved **my** mother once, a long time ago, but this isn't my mother. This is Harry's mother. My mother died years ago, it's just taken her body a while to catch up. What I understand now, looking at her, is that what hurts isn't that she treated me like shit at the end, it's that she treated me so well at the beginning. Had Mother always been the bitter and nasty woman that she has been since Harry died then I wouldn't be missing anything. But she wasn't, she was a good mother, a loving mother, she just got caught up in her own misery. It's incredibly easy to do, much easier in fact than actually dealing truthfully with life. I find now that what I want to do more than anything is to talk to her, to tell her that I finally get it. I want to tell her that she can be angry that Harry died as long as she realizes that I'm not dead, that I'm still here and I love her no matter what she says, or how angry she gets. I want to tell her that I'm sorry for not being here sooner, but I'm here now.

"Hey Johnny," I jump at the sound of Doctor Harris' voice, "I didn't mean to startle you."

"Oh, that's okay Doc, sometimes it's good to be startled, sort of like getting hit in the head with the life preserver, you know?"

"How's she doing?"

"Same as yesterday, and the day before, and last week…" Doctor Harris walks over to the foot of the bed and lifts the chart, the action reminds me of Dr. Richard Kiley from the Marcus Welby M.D. television show when I was a kid. A real hospital show, no blood and guts on the floor, cute nurses and nobody died.

"I know, would you mind coming outside for a minute?"

"Sure thing." I get up and follow Doctor Harris into the hall.

As I walk out of the room he closes the door behind me. "We're keeping her alive now John, she's not really contributing any more."

"Okay…so?" Dr, Harris shifts on his feet, and leans against the wall, we look like we're just two guys having a talk.

"So, I think you should talk to your father…" My heart drops, my mouth suddenly feels very dry, Dr. Harris continues "…I think we need to discontinue the medication."

"That's it?"

"It's the medicine for her kidneys that's keeping her alive John. If we stop administering it, they will shut down and she will die. We can make her comfortable, she won't be in any pain and odds are she won't even regain consciousness."

I start to shake; I raise my hand and look at it for a moment, the fingers twitching, a wave of nausea rising inside of me.

"Would..." I can't seem to focus, to get the words out. *What the fuck is going on? I didn't like this woman, Christ for the past few years I wasn't even sure I knew her. Now look at me.* "...How long would it take?"

"That I'm not sure of, a couple of hours, a few hours maybe. But no longer than twelve or fifteen I don't imagine."

"What if it does take longer?"

"Don't worry, it won't."

"I'm not worried; I just want to be able to explain this to my father!"

"Okay...okay John, I really don't believe she has more than a few hours in her, but if she makes more than twelve hours, we'll revisit the medications. I just think that given her age and that she has been largely unresponsive for some time it probably better to..."

"Pull the plug."

"I wouldn't say that John."

"But that's what we're doing isn't it?"

Doctor Harris pushes himself away from the wall, purses his lips for a moment and takes a pen from his pocket, "Yes, that is what we are doing. Will you speak with your father or will I?"

"I will, he should hear this from me." With that I walk down the hall, into the elevator, through the lobby and out to my car. Thirty minutes after that, in the den of their crummy apartment, sitting in the chair that my mother occupied for the last five years I tell my father that it is time for him to let mother go. He takes in a deep breath, let it out slowly and quietly nods his head.

"I don't want to be there."

"Okay...I'll go back." My father sighs again and hangs his head in his hands; I sand up, put my hand on his back and walk to the door. As open the door, I hear my father begin to cry.

Twenty-Four

———◆◆◆———

AT EIGHT THIRTY that night, in accordance with the orders of Dr. Donald J. Harris, Catherine Gros, R.N stopped the administration of all medication to my mother except for 1200 ccs of Demerol which were to be administered at the staff's discretion in order to keep my mother comfortable. When the nurse finally left, I got up, walked to the foot of the bed and after nearly a month of continuous noise finally turned the television off, returned to the chair next to my mother's bed and without thinking about anything at all, sat and waited.

At five thirty the next morning, on the Thursday before Thanksgiving, I watched my mother take three short breaths, seemingly trying reach out and catch it, her eyes opened briefly, then closed completely.

Mother then took one long deep breath, exhaled slowly and died.

Twenty-Five

---·••◆••·---

JANUARY SIXTH, THE day the Catholic Church observes as the visit of the Magi and also the official beginning of the New Orleans carnival season. This cold and blustery morning finds me sitting in a nineteen eighty-four Dodge Ram pick-up truck with a shitty paint job but one hell of a stereo that I got from a used car dealer out on Airline Highway who agreed to give me the truck and four grand in cash for my car. The bed of the truck is crammed with everything I thought of value; essentially just my books, my clothes, and ten signed New Orleans Jazz and Heritage posters all of it covered with a blue tarp that I have triple tied to the sides of the truck.

I gave up the rental house in December, breaking my lease and losing my damage deposit. I never went back to it after leaving the city to stay with my father while Mother was in the hospital, so whatever was in it was left to the next tenant. In fact since my mother died I have stayed away from any and all places that remind me of Jess, the pain and confusion of the last six months finally breaking through to me after Mother's memorial service.

I thought of selling my house on Jefferson, but went to Home Depot instead and invested in two truckloads of plywood and boarded it up. I left the keys with neighbors I barely knew, packed the Dodge and left.

I have to go. In a town famous for it mysticism, its grave yards and its haunting there are now far too many ghosts for me to bear. For the last two months I have discovered a weight that I have carried for a long time and I need to find a way to get rid of it, because here there are just too many places and things that remind me of love lost with no hope of return. I need to wash the slate clean, perhaps find some place that has no familiarity and no memories.

So now I sit in the truck across from the offices of the national advertising firm of J. Thomas Hunt and wait. I am waiting for the emergence of the smokers of the office who will at any time come out to the porch for their morning break. I take a drag on my own cigarette, burning it down to the filter before tossing it out of the driver's side window. After the cigarette hits the ground in a shower of sparks, I take the empty pack on the seat next to me crumple it up and toss it onto the floor of the truck on the passenger side, lean over to the glove box, open it and pull the box of transdermal patches out. I tear open the foil pouch, roll up my left sleeve, put the patch on my arm and immediately want another cigarette.

Five minutes later Jess walks out of the door with some of the others, they all carry coffee and they all light cigarettes. The winter morning light hits her red hair and explodes in color. She smiles, laughs and lacking a coat and wearing only a tank top she starts hopping back and forth in the cold air. The others with her disappear into a shroud of emotional haze as I focus solely on her and memorize each and every movement she makes until the cold apparently becomes too unbearable for her and she flicks her cigarette towards the street and bolts back inside the office.

I catch myself breathing short quick breaths, and tell myself to calm down. Finally after sitting quietly for a minute and full of the terror that tells me that I will never see her again and almost one year to the day after meeting the woman I will never have but never be without, I start the truck and head for the interstate.

Acknowledgements

There are an awful lot of people to which I am indebted for their help in telling this story.

Ms. Dorothy Grimm, my editor. Whose patience and encouragement as well as her grammatical skills turned this from nonsense to a novel.

My wife Maureen for being my final proofreader and more importantly for her patience and sense of humor in loving the writer in spite of what common sense may tell her.

My son Tucker who never gave up on me as a father, even when I would have given up on myself.

To Samantha Smith, whose friendship, encouragement and clumsiness started me on my way with this whole mess.

To my "favorite ex-wife" Jodi Nussbaum and her husband Kenny Cohen, for being the best extended family anyone could ask for.

To my friend, roommate and focus group for my early writing, Michelle Kaye Becker.

And..,

Finally to my family; my brother Don and sisters Carole, Peggy and Beck, for giving me love, a sense of humor and who were all there for our own parents way more than I was.

Breinigsville, PA USA
09 June 2010
239503BV00001B/66/P